DREAMER

~A FARAWAY HIGH FAIRYTALE~

SCARLETT KOL

The characters in this book are fictitious. Any similarity to real persons, living or dead, places, or events is coincidental and not intended by author.

DREAMER
Copyright © 2020 by Scarlett Kol
All rights reserved.

ISBN: (ebook) 978-1-7752260-4-8
Print: 978-1-7752260-5-5
First Edition: 2019

Edited by Laura Parnum
www.LauraParnumBooks.com

Cover Art by Sanja Gombar

Author Photo by Regina Wamba

No part of this book may be reproduced in any form or by any electronic or mechanical means, including information storage and retrieval systems, without written permission from the author, except for the use of brief quotations in a book review.

Published by Vicious Pixie Press

*To those who believe in fairytales
and chasing their dreams.*

"He declared that he loved her better than he loved himself."

- Charles Perrault,
The Sleeping Beauty in the Wood

Translated: A. E. Johnson
(dodd mead and company, 1921)

1

———

Once upon a time, I knew everything.

I knew exactly who I was (Breanne Vardan, honor roll student since kindergarten), where I was going (Princeton), and how I was going to get there (scholarships, student loans, and working summers at the Twisted Top ice cream parlor). But my whole life had been a dream. A sweet illusion. Until the day I fell asleep and everything changed. That day, I finally woke up.

This morning, though, I wasn't even tired. Glorious sunshine lit my path as leaves in every color from the Starbucks specialty coffee menu drifted through the air. I breathed in the aesthetic, letting it warm my skin against the cool October breeze. If only Mother Nature could've saved this weather for the weekend instead of just a Thursday—but maybe she knew that today was a special day.

I pulled open one of the glass front doors of Faraway

High, then unwrapped my scarf, leaving the long ends to dangle from my neck. Bodies floated past through the halls, barely noticing another person joining their ranks for the daily routine of classes, classes, and more classes before being released back into the world. The roller-coaster of infamy and anonymity of high school life.

My cell phone buzzed in my pocket.

Aunt Becky: Make sure to come straight home after school today. Love you.

Of course, I would. I always did. She just worried way too much. I clicked the thumbs-up emoji and hit send, then took the first staircase to the second floor. I meandered down the hall of lockers, taking each step slowly. Only a few students lurked up here this early, even though class started in a half hour. The luxury of living in a small town meant never having to rush, but I liked sneaking away to the calm before the chaos of the school day started. If you wanted to be seen, you stayed on the main floor. Upstairs was purely functional visits only. Just the keeners, the loners, and the lost up here in the morning, soaking up the quiet. Plus, it gave me space to review my notes before class.

At the far end of the hall, I finally reached my locker and started spinning the combination in the lock. A strange voice echoed around me. A whisper. I stopped turning and looked back down the hall. No one looked up. I shook my head. Must be dreaming.

I finished the combination and popped the locker open. Rainbow balloons burst out at me and I screamed, then jumped backward. They floated up near the ceiling and bobbed there, tethered by blue ribbons taped to the inside of my locker door.

"Happy birthday!" Sasha, Ainsley, and Cora popped out from beside the locker bank, tossing thin streamers and blowing annoying party horns.

I laughed and flung my right hand over my face as red heat exploded in my cheeks. Chuckles and comments streamed from down the hall at the spectacle. Great. Just perfect.

"Now, every birthday girl needs a crown." Sasha pulled a silver sequined and faux fur tiara from behind her back, the words "Best Birthday Ever" in the center. She plunked it on my head and Ainsley quickly snapped a picture before I could hide.

"You guys are awful, you know that?" As I pulled the tiara from my head, the combs toward the back ripped out a few pieces of my hair. I shook the crown made for a toddler out in front of me, letting the golden strands flutter to the floor. "And I'm not wearing this all day."

"No worries. We have all the proof we need." Ainsley tapped the side of her phone and slipped it into her Go Lions backpack. "Besides, you totally love us."

"Yeah, I do."

"Happy birthday, Brea." Sasha circled in for a hug and I squeezed her tight as the smell of her vanilla shampoo wafted over my face.

"But you have to tell her the other news." Cora clapped her hands, her deep green eyes twinkling with excitement.

"Easy. I'll get there." Sasha released me and winked. "Okay, we're there. I'm throwing you a birthday party tomorrow night."

A squeal escaped my lips. "Really?"

"Yep. My parents are going to St. Louis for some work conference and said that I could throw you a birthday party as long as Lev stays home to watch over us."

"That's so amazing. Thank you."

"Well," she took my hand and swung my arm, "you're my best friend, and you only get one sweet sixteen. I want it to be special."

"Ah. You're the best." I hugged her again, my feet tapping on the floor.

Cora raised an eyebrow. "Plus, you want to throw a huge shaker when your parents aren't home."

Sasha laughed. "Maybe that too. But only if you wear the crown."

She snagged the tiara from my hand and stuck it back on my head.

"Not a chance."

"Meh." She shrugged. "I'm still having the party. Maybe I'll even invite Malcolm Rogers."

Malcolm Rogers? Handsome, smart, charming, senior Malcolm Rogers?

I cleared my throat and swallowed the bubble of excitement trying to force its way out of my mouth. "Go ahead. You're throwing the party. Invite whoever you want."

"And you just won't care if he's there or not? Even though as soon as I mentioned his name your face caught fire faster than a polyester skirt soaked in gasoline?"

I looked down at the beige floor tiles, counting the

brown speckles as the burn hit the tops of my ears. "I wouldn't complain if he showed up or anything."

Sasha laughed. "All right, ladies, let's leave Brea alone to fantasize about her dream wedding to Malcolm and go spread the word about this party."

The three of them paraded off down the hall. Hurricane Sasha and her twin tropical storms trailing behind in skinny jeans. Ever since Sasha blew into town in first grade, she'd been my best friend. She didn't make fun of me about my parents when the other kids did, loved My Little Ponies, and always managed to push me out of my comfort zone, if only by a toe. Yin to my horribly boring yang. Ainsley and Cora hopped on for the ride somewhere in middle school, but Sasha and I, we clicked.

"Why do you and your friends always have to be so pink and sparkly?"

I blinked a couple of times and snapped back into the present, the annoying monotone of Declan Noche breaking me out of my pleasant memories. I glanced down at my outfit. Black leggings and a purple dress. Clearly not pink. Maybe he needed to get his eyes tested. Or maybe being condescending got him extra credit in some weird human studies class.

"And why do you have to be all this—" I snickered and waved my open palm in a circle toward him. His black-on-black outfit might pass as early excitement for Halloween, if he didn't wear it 365 days a year. Granted, the way his T-shirt pulled against his thick arms worked for him, but seriously, a pop of color would be nice once in a while, "—what is that exactly? Rockstar reject, maybe? Or are you trying out to be a shadow in the school play or something?"

"Funny."

He pulled out a textbook with a pristine spine that had likely never been cracked, and scanned me over from my toes to my forehead with his complicated dark eyes. I'd care, except he always did this. The broody "I'm-so-intense" thing. Not even two months into the school year and it was already exhausting. Every morning he'd start the snarky banter, and every day I'd dish it back. Kind of entertaining, but when he started down the throwback emo road, I got bored.

I shoved the ridiculous tiara in the back of my locker and ran my fingers through my hair, trying to salvage some of my curls. I hadn't mentioned my birthday, but it didn't mean I didn't celebrate by spending a few more minutes in front of the mirror this morning working some meticulous curling iron magic. Sixteen. Less than two years until I could get out of this town and start building my future.

"I'm guessing it's your birthday, then?"

I leaned back and looked at him again. *Could this guy read minds or something?* "Yep. What tipped you off?"

He pointed at the balloons still hovering above my locker, dipping up and down in the hallway drafts.

"Oh, right. I forgot those were up there." I tugged on the ribbons and shoved the balloons back into my locker, slamming the door so they couldn't escape.

"Well then—" the perma-sneer curl of his lip diminished to what looked like an attempt at a genuine smile, "—happy birthday."

I waited for the punch line, but it never came. Just his big, beaming grin and a bizarre tingle rippling across my skin.

"Thanks."

"I don't know why people make such a big deal about them. It's just a day. Everyone has them. Just another reminder of how old you're getting."

My shoulders sank. And . . . Declan was back to being Declan. Broody, moody, and oh so cynical.

"Then I guess I won't have to tell you where my massive birthday party is, since you wouldn't want me to invite you anyway."

He scoffed and closed his locker, then turned and fell back against it, trying too hard to look all careless and aloof. "Of course not. I've got better things to do."

"Right. Some sort of army boot convention in town?"

He assessed his shoes, turning his ankle out, then grinned. "Yeah, something like that."

I leaned my shoulder against the locker, matching his slightly diagonal stance but without the attitude. "But I guess if you did want to come, I'd tell you that it's tomorrow night at Sasha's, just past the edge of town. Not like it matters."

"Yeah. Not like it matters." Declan rolled onto his right shoulder until we stood face to face, his wavy hair flopping over his forehead and blending with his thick, dark lashes. "But if I did want to come, I know where it is."

"Good. I'd pretend to be intimidated by this whole wannabe-bad-boy thing you're working, but let's be honest. We live in Iowa. The worst thing that's ever happened around here was that fight after homecoming, and it turned out fine. I doubt you're as much trouble as you think you are."

His lips curled up into a crooked smile—an expression I'd rarely seen since we'd met. He pushed his weight into his shoulder and bounced off the locker so that he stood upright again. He backed away slowly, his stare still locked on my face.

"Oh, Brea, you don't even know."

2

As I pushed open the side door of my house, my mouth watered, raw and uninhibited like an animal. Garlic, parmesan, and the heavy, greasy smell of extra cheese. If someone were lurking inside to kidnap me, I'd go willingly, as long as they let me have whatever created that decadent aroma.

"Hey there, kid. Happy birthday," Aunt Becky called from the kitchen.

I slipped off my shoes and headed up the three steps to the tile floor. Aunt Becky stood in her impeccably tidy skirt suit, hunched over the sink, washing green leaves of romaine under the running tap. I leaned against the counter and crossed my arms, inhaling the scent and peeking at the steam rising from the casserole dish on the other side of the kitchen. "Dinner's a bit early today?"

She looked up from the sink and wiped the back of her wet hand across her brow. A stray blond hair slid behind her ear, the only escaped strand from the bun tightly wound at the nape of her neck. "Well, I'm working the overnight manager shift at the inn tonight, but I didn't want to miss dinner with the birthday girl. I made your favorite. Lasagna. I hope that's okay."

"More than okay. I'm starving."

She smiled at her hands full of lettuce. "It's almost ready. If you could just take the garlic bread from the oven, we can eat."

I grabbed an oven mitt and slid the pan of bread out of the oven. Cheese bubbled over the perfectly toasted sides, and my stomach gurgled in appreciation. I quickly transferred the hot slices onto a plate then stuck my index finger in my mouth to suck away the pain of a slight burn.

The side door creaked open. Tori hurried in and whisked off her dark green trench coat. She swung it onto a hook, then leapt over the steps to join us in the kitchen.

"You're off early?" I said, as I set out the plates and cutlery on the quilted placemats.

She flipped her black curls over her shoulder and straightened her blouse with a slight shimmy, shaking off the rest of the day. "I couldn't miss a birthday dinner with my best girls, now, could I? So, I worked through my lunch and just took off a little early. Happy birthday, Brea." She raised her arms and I obliged her with a hug, her strong biceps nearly squeezing my bones through my skin. She let go, then slipped over to Aunt Becky and gave her a sweet welcome-home kiss while I pretended not to notice.

I placed the garlic bread on the table and took my

seat, pinching a slice for myself and dropping it on my plate.

Aunt Becky and Tori brought over the salad and the main dish and joined me at the table with twin smiles.

"So how does it feel to be sweet sixteen?" Aunt Becky said, serving up the amazing-looking lasagna. Sauce and cheese oozed off the spatula and my mouth salivated, waiting impatiently for a taste. Her pink lipstick grin widened at my desperation.

"Not much different than yesterday. However, I can't wait to start driving."

"Why? So you can drive the three streets in this map-dot town?" Tori laughed. "Walking is probably faster around here."

"Maybe, but at least I'd be able to go somewhere other than Faraway."

"Don't get too ahead of yourself. You still have to pass your driver's test. And last I checked, you didn't have a car," Aunt Becky pointed her finger at me, "so unless you plan on buying one, you might be a little less uninhibited than you expected."

"Or, I might just have the best aunt in the world who will lend me her Pontiac once in a while?" I batted my lashes at her and tilted my head to the side.

She burst into laughter. "Baby steps, Brea. Let's get that license first before you start planning cross-country road trips."

I pierced my fork through the layers of cheese and noodles then stuffed the too-big piece in my mouth. Perfect. The rich, thick sauce blended with creamy spinach, and it seemed like Aunt Becky had sprung for the expensive mozzarella. I took another bite, my angry stomach finally starting to chill after the second helping. Forks scraped porcelain. The low murmur of satisfied moans rumbled through the kitchen. Aunt Becky should quit the inn and open her own diner or something, or at least find a job where her talents weren't wasted working midnights behind a desk.

"This is amazing, like always. Best birthday present ever." I smeared the extra tomato sauce across my plate with the garlic bread, not willing to waste a drop of the saucy goodness.

Aunt Becky wiped her mouth with a napkin and cringed as she swallowed. "This isn't your present. I hadn't gotten to that part yet." She glanced over at Tori who smiled back and put down her fork, her hands propped underneath her chin to listen. "We got you a little something, but we figured since you're getting older it would likely be better if you just picked out the rest of your gift yourself."

"Yeah, way to ruin a surprise, girl," Tori added.

Aunt Becky raced over to the counter and pulled out a small purple box from behind the cookie jar. "Here."

I opened the box. Inside, a beautiful silver coin sat on a chain. The letter B was etched in the center.

"I love it. Thanks so much." I slipped it from the box and clipped it around my neck, then let it fall around my collarbone.

"I'm glad you like it." Aunt Becky sat back down. "So, tomorrow after school we'll all head to Des Moines, go shopping, get our nails done, and hit up that new Mexican restaurant, Chiquita's."

I shrank down in my chair, the temperature in the

room skyrocketing. "Would you mind if we went on Saturday?"

Aunt Becky frowned, her face scrunching up tight. "Why? Is there something going on?"

"It's just that Sasha kinda wanted to throw me a birthday party tomorrow, and I was kinda of planning to go since she's doing it for me."

Aunt Becky's head started to shake before the words came out of her mouth. "And let me guess. Her parents aren't home, are they?"

"No, but her older brother Lev will be there. He's nineteen and totally responsible."

"Nope. No way. You're not going to some wild party to get into who knows what kind of trouble."

"Aunt Becky, this is Sasha. You've known Sasha since she was six years old. If you are that worried, you can even drive by since it's only, like, fifteen minutes away." I yanked my napkin off my lap and tossed it on the table. "Please. You never let me do anything."

"Of course I do. You don't even understand how lucky of a girl you are. There are so many other kids out there who would beg to have the life you have."

"Don't try this with me, Aunt Becky. It's not that I'm not grateful for what I have, but you just won't let me grow up. I'm never allowed to do things without you."

"That's not true."

"Sophomore ski trip, you didn't let me go."

She shrugged and started poking at her lasagna, avoiding eye contact. "You hate snow. I just did you a favor."

"Spring break trip with Ainsley and her parents to Daytona Beach. Didn't let me go."

"It was last minute. I didn't have it in the budget. Besides, think of all that money you saved for college instead."

I kicked my chair back and stood up, slamming my palms against the table top. "I can't believe you. It's just a party. Do you even know the kind of stuff that kids my age are doing? They're doing drugs and vaping, and talking to strangers on the Internet, and posting half-naked pictures of themselves on social media. I'm not doing any of those things. I work hard and I'm a good kid. Why can't I just go to one party for my own birthday?"

She kept twirling her fork in front of her, her eyes glued to the stainless steel tines. Her voice dropped. "It's not happening. And that's final."

"You are so unreasonable."

I marched out of the kitchen and through the living room, then stomped up the stairs.

"Breanne Rosalie Vardan, you get back here right now."

I bit my tongue, fighting the urge to scream "no," and kept stomping. At the end of the hall I slammed my bedroom door behind me. A twinge of guilt crept up my back for acting like a four-year-old and probably proving Aunt Becky's point that I couldn't be responsible, but the whip of my arm and the hollow sound echoing down the hall did feel pretty good.

She was unbelievable. High school students go to parties. It's kind of a thing. But no, not me. Not with Aunt Becky watching over me like a warden. Normally we got along great, but she just couldn't let me go. Ever.

The shelves over my desk could barely hold the

ribbons and trophies and certificates from all the things I'd accomplished. Spelling bees, honor roll, track meets —anything they could give an award for, I was there with a smile and a ton of hard work to back it up. I'd always worked like crazy. Didn't I deserve a little bit of fun now and again? I flopped onto my bed and clutched my fluffy star pillow in my arms, picking at the yellow fur. What was I even going to tell Sasha? Thanks for throwing me the biggest rager of my life, but I don't think I'm gonna make it? It was so stupid.

The outside door slammed downstairs as Aunt Becky left for work. I took a deep breath and exhaled slowly, trying to let the anger go. But it wouldn't change anything anyway.

I fell back and stared at the ceiling. The tiny peaks of the stucco stared back down.

Why couldn't I just get to be normal for once?

A quiet knock rapped on the bedroom door.

"Who is it?"

Tori didn't answer. Instead she pushed open the door and let herself in. Her eyes looked strained and tired and my stomach pinched, knowing at least part of her stress came from me.

"I brought cake." Tori pulled two small plates topped with gooey chocolate slabs out from behind her back and forced a smile. "It's bad luck not to eat cake on your birthday."

She handed me a slice and sat down cross-legged at the foot of the bed, balancing her own plate on her knee.

I picked off a few pink sprinkles from the icing and licked them off my finger. "She made the double fudge devil's food with whipped ganache frosting, didn't she?"

She nodded, and my entire body wilted like a daisy in the fall.

"You know she'd do anything for you, right? She loves you that much."

"I know. And I love her too, but you've seen how she gets. She never lets me do anything. She's so overprotective, like one day she might just lock me away like a princess in a tower. It's hard to breathe sometimes, you know?"

Tori put the cake down on the navy blue bedspread and slid closer to rub my shoulder. "Yeah, I know. She can be a bit much, but it's only because she worries about you. And you don't have to fret, because I think locking people in towers is illegal in this state."

I tried not to laugh, but a chuckle slipped out.

She continued, "When your parents disappeared and the lawyer brought you to live with her, you should have seen Becks freaking out. You were four years old, but you'd think they'd handed her a newborn with no instruction manual. And since then, she's been doing the best that she knows how. She's not trying upset you."

"I don't think she's doing a bad job. I just need some freedom. I'm not that four-year-old kid anymore. In less than two years I'm going to leave for college, and how's she going to deal with that? Is she planning to move into my dorm?"

Tori giggled then took another bite of cake. "Don't give her the option. But, she knows you'll leave her soon and she's just trying to hold on for a little longer. Me and you—" she swayed toward me and gave me a playful punch in the chin, "—we're her whole world."

I stared down at the plate, running my fingernail

along the worn gold trim. She loved me. I got it. But why did she have to make it so difficult?

"Want to know a secret?"

I glanced up.

"The night they brought you to Becks's apartment, she had a total nervous breakdown. She swore there was no way she'd ever be able to raise her brother's kid. She said she didn't even want kids. Thought they were dirty and smelly."

I laughed. "They kinda are."

"Yeah, they totally are. She had even rehearsed her speech to tell the lawyer to take you back, but the second she opened that door and saw those big blue eyes staring up at her from under the most god-awful bangs, she knew you needed to stay."

An invisible weight settled against my ribs. "She was going to give me up?"

"Maybe for like half a second. But clearly someone needed to save you from that awful, awful haircut."

"Thanks, but I'd rather have nasty bangs than miss out on my own birthday party."

Tori sighed. "I'll talk to her. You're growing up too fast for us, Brea. But, maybe I can convince her to lighten up a little bit. You just have to promise to not take advantage of it if she starts to give you some room."

"Really? Thank you so much." I gave her a huge squeeze and she patted me on the back.

"I'm not promising anything." She slipped off the bed and sashayed back toward the door. "So, are you gonna spend your whole birthday hanging out in your room and pouting, or do you want to binge some '90s melodrama and help me polish off half a cake?"

"Sure. Just give me a minute and I'll be right down."

The door clicked closed behind her, and her footsteps padded down the hall. I rubbed my hands over my face, the heavy scent of chocolate still on my fingertips. Hopefully, Tori could work some magic with Aunt Becky or I'd have to come up with some amazing story for school tomorrow.

I got out of bed and leaned on the window frame. The blood-red sun dipped low and kissed the edge of the horizon. The sun setting on sweet sixteen.

Happy birthday to me.

3

If y = 3x⁵ – 5x³ – 2x² – 1, then what is— $If\ y = 3x^5 - 5x^3 - 2x^2 - 1,\ then\ what\ is—$ Sasha yanked the book away from my face and snapped it shut with a thud.

"Hey. I was reading that."

"My parents are officially gone." Sasha fell into the chair across from me and leaned her elbows across the table. "Lev is hiding all the breakables as we speak. This is going to be the best party of the year." She turned the book in her hand and read the spine, her nose twitching as she frowned. "And why aren't you more excited? It's Friday. Birthday party day."

I grabbed the book from her and tucked it under my arm on the table. "And Friday I-have-a-quiz-in-second-period day."

"So you're skipping class to study? Sounds kinda backward."

"No, I have a spare first period because of the extra credit project I did for Mr. Sebastian last fall. You're the one who's skipping class."

"Better study harder, because you're wrong." She slipped a folded piece of paper out of her pocket and waved it in the air. "I have a note. My parents wanted me to see them off to the airport, so it's not skipping. It's an excused absence."

I shook my head. "Lev wrote it, didn't he?"

"Maybe. But no one's going to bother to prove it. Besides, I had to promise to clean all the bathrooms before and after the party for this." She snapped the letter against her open palm. "And I repeat, it's birthday party day. Why aren't you more excited?"

I rested my chin on the textbook and glanced around at the empty mid-'70s flowered couches in the student lounge. "My aunt isn't super happy about the party. She really doesn't want me to go."

"What?" Her palms slammed down, making the whole table shake. "But you are coming, right?"

"Yeah. She said I could, but I have to be in my house at midnight."

"Seriously? Are we suddenly living in some sort of fairy tale? Your aunt has always been too much, but it's starting to border on cruel. Is she trying to keep you sheltered before she sells you off to the convent or something?"

"I don't think people get sold to a convent. I think they go willingly."

The school bell rang and I shot up in my seat. Sasha rolled her eyes and turned toward the hallway door, examining her shiny plum manicure.

"Well, I would be kicking and screaming the whole way. Did you tell her my brother was going to be there? He can vote, so he qualifies as an adult."

"Yeah, no luck. Tori had to beg her to let me go at all. Plus, apparently 'nothing good happens after midnight.'"

Her hazel eyes twinkled. I'd seen this look before. The one she always sported before she convinces me to do something insane. "Your aunt is totally wrong there. The best things happen after midnight."

I sighed and packed my calculus text into my bag. "You know what she means."

"I know. Just wanted you to cheer up. If you'll turn into a pumpkin at midnight, then I guess we'll just have to start as early as possible."

"Thanks, Sasha. I know it's a pain, but I can't risk it."

We both stood from the table, and she tossed her arm over my shoulder. "It's fine. She's not going to change overnight, but if this goes well, maybe she'll ease up a bit."

"Here's hoping."

"Okay, Ainsley and Cora will be at my place at six to help set up, so get there as soon as you can, and I'll spread the word that doors are opening early." She winked, then backed down the hall, hitting a cheerleader and nearly taking out the quiet guy from the back row of my science class.

I shook my head and shuffled off in the other direction, trying to solve the interrupted equation in my head.

"Hey, Brea."

If I divide x by . . .

"I said, hey, Brea." A thick male hand waved in front of my face and I jerked back into the moment. "I heard there's going to be a huge birthday bash for you over at the McKenzie's place tonight."

Tiny black spots clouded my vision. I blinked. The hallway lights made it hard to focus, or maybe it was because I couldn't believe that Malcolm Rogers was trying to get my attention. Malcolm. Talking to me. Not around me. Not to a group I happened to be in. To me. About my party.

"Yeah, Sasha is throwing it for me." The words came out flat, like one of the voices on those dated driver's ed videos they'd been showing us in class, but I couldn't stop them. The stunned feeling that coursed through my body seemed to make my tongue go numb.

Malcolm rested his arm against the wall in front of me, crossing his feet and staring into me. His green eyes dragged me in like black holes. I tried to grab onto solid ground, but they pulled harder, as if they knew exactly what they were doing.

His lip curled up into a mischievous half-smile. "Mind if I maybe come by?"

I leaned against the wall, not for effect, but to keep my knees from dropping me to the tile floor. "I'm sure it would be fine. I mean, yeah, it would be awesome if you came."

"Cool." His smile deepened, his teeth poking out from behind his lips. My face flushed like an idiot. He pushed off the wall. "Then I'll see you tonight."

He swaggered past me and I tilted my head to watch him walk away, my brain still spinning as his broad shoulders maneuvered through the swarm of students trying to get to class. I closed my eyes, then breathed deep and exhaled. That was ridiculous. Me acting so stupid over a boy. Sure, he looked like an underwear model, all chiseled jaw and dreamy pensive expressions, but if I'd only had a couple minutes to prepare, I could've put together more cohesive thoughts instead of acting like I'd been drugged up for dental surgery. I rubbed my sweaty hands over my thighs and shook my head. I'd have to be more in control next time. More composed. And there would be a next time since Malcolm Rogers was coming to my party. *My* birthday party. Sasha was never going to believe this.

"So, you and the fabulous Malcolm Rogers? Faraway's newest power couple?"

I turned back. Declan stood in front of me in the hall.

My dreamy thoughts fell from the clouds and crash-landed at my feet as I waited for his inevitable sarcasm to pop my bubble of happiness. "Why are you always lurking around?"

He scoffed and rolled his eyes toward the ceiling, his knuckles going white as he gripped the lone book tighter in his fist. "Me? Lurking? Not exactly. This school is so small I would've heard your conversation even if I wasn't already standing right here. Or maybe you were too star struck over pretty-boy Malcolm to notice anyone else walking by?"

I continued down the hall, and as I passed, Declan locked step with me.

"What's your issue with Malcolm? I'm sure you have some sort of opinion on the matter. Not like it's any of your business."

He looked back over his shoulder after Malcolm, his face contorting to a nasty snarl. "It's just he's . . . I don't know . . ."

"Not my type?"

"Oh, he's definitely your type. Preppy, delightful, and kind of shiny."

"Then what's your problem?"

The second period bell rang and he huffed as the hall began to clear. He banged his hand against a nearby locker door, making me jump as the clang of metal echoed into the distance and disappeared.

"Because, Brea," he pulled his book across his chest and started to walk in the other direction, "you can't see that you deserve way better."

4

"I'll be back for you right at midnight, not a minute later." Tori gripped the steering wheel with her left hand and shook a perfectly French-manicured finger at me with her right. "If you mess this up, Becks will never forgive me and you can pretty much expect to live with us forever."

"Thank you, Tori. I won't let you down." I grabbed onto her bicep and nuzzled my head against her shoulder in a makeshift hug, then launched out of the passenger seat and closed the door behind me.

She slowly pulled out of the driveway as I stood in front of Sasha's house and took a deep breath. I pinched my tight magenta dress and shimmied it farther down my thighs. Aunt Becky had nearly collapsed when I walked out in this dress, but other than the tight skirt, everything else was covered and flowy. It even had long sleeves. Besides, what was wrong with looking hot now and again? Seriously, someone needed to get her to relax.

Music pumped through the closed windows, getting louder as I approached the doorstep. I rang the bell, not sure if anyone would even hear it, but Sasha immediately appeared and rushed me inside.

"Where have you been?" she asked, her hands on her hips and a worried frown across her face. Her concern didn't quite match her outfit—a sparkly black tank top and ripped crop jeans that made her look like some off-duty runway model looking for a fun time.

"Sorry. I didn't want to upset my aunt, so I kinda waited around for the right moment to leave."

"Did she say you could stay any later?"

"No. She even stood in the window like some creepy gargoyle watching us pull out of the driveway. But Tori said she would pick me up at my curfew, which means I don't have to be out of here any earlier."

Her narrowed eyes softened and she squeezed me tight. "Well, at least you made it. Lev's friends have been here since I got home after school, and people have been texting that they will be coming soon. I have no idea how many people are going to be here, but I think it might be a school record."

"Plus, Malcolm Rogers stopped me in the hall today and asked if he could come."

Her perfectly red-lined lips dropped wide open. "Seriously? He actually said he'd show up?"

I nodded, a goofy grin breaking across my face.

"I guess this party is an even better birthday present than I planned."

"Yes, and thank you so much. You have no idea how much it means to me that you would do this."

She shrugged and her high ponytail whipped back

and forth. "Well, even if it wasn't your birthday, there is never a bad reason to have a party. Ainsley and Cora are in the kitchen if you want to help them finish setting up."

Sasha pointed toward the kitchen as if I hadn't been here a thousand times before. However, even though this sometimes felt like a second home, the huge windows and clean lines always took my breath away. Sasha's dad had designed everything and traded work from his architecture firm to have it built. It was one of the biggest houses in Faraway, or actually near Faraway, as it stood down a private road just past the town line. The open views looked out into the wild forest, where not even the light from another house could be seen. We'd spent hours running through those woods, Sasha and I, pretending to be princesses or witches, or sometimes even unicorns. But that all seemed so long ago.

"Hey, it's the birthday girl," Cora announced as I entered the kitchen. Ainsley waved from her perch on the kitchen counter, pulling red plastic cups from a bag and lining them up in towers beside her. Bowls of chips and pretzels covered the island, yet to be deployed to the other rooms of the house.

"When did you guys get here?" I asked, grabbing another sleeve of cups and ripping open the plastic bag.

"Ainsley came right after school, but I just got here about twenty minutes ago," Cora said. She poured a bag of ice into a large silver cooler sitting on the floor, the chunks tinkling against the cans and bottles already inside.

"Yeah, Sasha's been freaking out about this whole thing all week and I wanted to make sure that it went okay." Ainsley pushed off the edge of the counter and fluttered down to the tile floor, her blue halter top flashing just an inch of skin above the waist of her jeans. She pulled me into a hug then straightened the top of my dress. "You look amazing, Brea. Happy birthday."

"Thanks. And you two look fantastic, like always. I love your bracelet, Cora. Is it new? I've never seen it before."

Cora held her wrist up toward the kitchen light, the tiny charms glinting on the chain. "Yeah. I got it for my birthday, two weeks ago." She forced an awkward smile, barely masking the harsh edge in her tone.

I glanced at Ainsley. She shrugged, then looked down at her stack of cups and went back to work. For Cora's birthday we did dinner and a movie, and everyone ended up bailing early because of homework.

An apology started to slide up my throat but lodged around my tonsils as I tried to choke it back down. Sorrys weren't what she needed and would probably make her feel worse. "So, it's almost like a party for both our birthdays. That's even better."

She scoffed. "Yeah, right." She ripped open another bag of ice, the chill rolling off her colder than the cooler. She closed her eyes and sighed. "But don't worry about it. I know you and Sasha have been best friends for way longer. It makes sense."

Ainsley grabbed three cups from the top of the closest tower and pulled a black sharpie from her back pocket. She wrote "All hail the goddess" on one and then "Kiss me, it's my birthday" on the other two with a few streamers and black balloons to finish the look.

"Thanks, but I doubt that cup will make much of a difference."

"You never know," Ainsley said. "Lots of things can happen at a party. Besides, I invited the whole cheer squad to come tonight, and if Captain Kate decides to make an appearance, then everyone else from school will be here too."

"Do you really think Kate is going to come to a junior party?" Cora asked. "You're still only an alternate, remember."

"Well, I'm hoping that if she comes tonight it will help that situation. Besides, there's nothing else going on in town, so if she's looking for something to do, she might just come and bring crashers." Ainsley clapped her hands and gave a high-pitched squeal.

"Crashers? Do you think Sasha will be mad?"

"Hell no," Cora murmured from below the counter as she organized the final bag of ice. "You know how Sasha loves the drama."

"Good point."

Ainsley grabbed a tall can from the cooler and wiped off the excess water, then popped the tab and split it between the three cups. She handed me and Cora our birthday cups then hoisted her own in cheers. We clinked our plastic cups together.

"What is this?" I asked, eyeing the pink carbonated liquid in the cup.

Ainsley cleared her throat, her hand at her collarbone. "Does it really matter? It tastes amazing."

I took a sip. Watermelon-flavored bubbles tickled my throat, and my nose twitched.

Ainsley took a large gulp of her own drink then

draped her arm around my shoulder, leading me back out of the kitchen. "I have a feeling tonight's going to be a night you will always remember."

I CHECKED MY CELL PHONE: 10:59. In the hours that flew by, Sasha's house had transformed from cavernous museum to practically a nightclub, assuming this was what a nightclub looked like from the inside.

Cans and bottles littered the tables and even the floor. Fog clouded the huge picture windows as the house temperature rose almost ten degrees every time someone new arrived. Most of the cheerleading squad had shown up, as Ainsley had hoped, which brought even more people as the night raced by. Fortunately, with all the bodies around, it would be easier to slip out without being noticed. Except, the more people that showed, the less I wanted to leave.

Most of the guests didn't really know me well, but I enjoyed watching them all. Everyone talking, drinking, and laughing as if tonight was the only thing on their minds. They pressed against each other, not caring if anyone saw, though they probably should. Even with the cool October chill, a few seniors braved Sasha's pool on the deck, and their cheers echoed through the main part of the house. All in all, Sasha could consider this party a total success. I just wished I could stay.

I took another sip of my drink and cringed. It flowed lukewarm and flat down my throat. The bubbles had long since popped, and it tasted more like the metal can it had come in than watermelon. I swirled the liquid around the still-half-filled cup and considered ditching it in the kitchen, but at least carrying it around gave me an excuse when Ainsley kept insisting on trying to get me a new one. I'd already risked Aunt Becky's wrath by coming tonight, I didn't need to add to her disappointment.

"How has that been working for you?"

A familiar voice spoke behind me and I spun around to come face to face with Malcom Rogers, his index finger pointing at my cup. My throat suddenly dried like I'd swallowed sandpaper, and I quickly took another sip to facilitate my vocal cords. His strong cologne knocked me in the face, and I held the side of my head to stop the dizzy sensation running through my brain. I regained control as his lips curled into an amused smile.

"This?" I held the cup higher for him to see. "Hasn't really had much of an impact, but I wouldn't want to kiss half the people here anyway."

He laughed, his shoulders heaving in time with the sound. "Then I guess that means there are some people here you might want to kiss."

My entire body heated, aflame as if his words had struck a match. And they kinda had.

"Maybe. If the right offer came along."

"I'll have to remember that. Are you having a happy birthday?"

"Yeah. Sasha sure knows how to throw a party."

"Definitely. But kinda loud, don't you think?" He scanned the room, his nose wrinkling as his eyes darted from face to face. "Did you want to go out on the deck where it's a bit quieter?"

I nodded, all the vocabulary words I'd practiced for my PSATs failing me. *Get it together, Brea.*

He led me through the chaos—people dancing, people standing, people sitting—and I followed until we hit the glass door off the living room. He swung the door out and held it open for me to pass, forcing me to slide close to him on the way through, which I didn't mind at all.

He shut the door behind us. The noise level plummeted thousands of decibels, and as the party haze lifted from my mind, I could think again. I took a few more steps out onto the wide deck and into the calm night, staring out into the dark forest just beyond the edge of the perfectly manicured lawn. Stars dotted the sky like sparklers lit just for me, their bluish-white light creating shadows under the boughs of the trees that danced and swayed in the late-night breeze. Malcolm leaned against the railing and looked out into Sasha's woods, his fingers knuckle-white. I crossed my arms and pulled them closer as the chill on my bare legs prickled my skin.

"It's kind of a beautiful night, don't you think?" I asked, trying to fill the empty space between us.

He pulled back from the rail and looked over at me as his playful eyes pinned mine. "Maybe. But I think I found something even more beautiful."

He swept his hand across my hair, his pinky finger tracing the top of my ear. Shivers splintered through my limbs and I flinched. He smiled, then glanced down, grabbing the back of his neck. The soft moonlight painted highlights through his short, dirty-blond hair.

"Sorry. I saw you standing there, and I just . . . I don't know."

"It's okay. I don't think there's any girl that doesn't like being called beautiful."

"And I'm sure you get that all the time."

I raised my left eyebrow, my face scrunching up. Tori, Aunt Becky, and I had watched enough vintage low-budget romances to know this was a line, and not a particularly good one. Maybe he lacked creativity. Or maybe he was nervous?

"Not exactly," I said.

"Well, you should." He took my cup and put it on the small outdoor coffee table next to Sasha's wicker couch, then slid his left hand into mine. "It's been really hard not to notice you lately. You are so smart, and sweet. You put most of the girls in the senior class to shame."

Another line. "Thanks, but I—"

He rested his right hand under my chin and pulled my head up as he leaned closer.

What? It was this easy? I'd expected to talk more, or to go somewhere else where people weren't vaping in the far corner. Before yesterday I wasn't even sure he knew my name, and after barely five minutes he expected me to make out with him in front of the entire school? And maybe I should. So many other girls would. Why couldn't I be more like them?

I closed my eyes, but a sharp pain shot through my stomach as my brain twisted my organs in knots. I'd pictured kissing Malcolm more times than I would even admit to myself, but now, with him edging closer, it felt all wrong.

"Hey," I pulled my hand from his and dropped down

off my tiptoes, "I never offered you a drink. Did you want to maybe go get one with me?"

He retracted his face and I pointed toward the kitchen, each word out of my mouth sounding dumber than the last.

Malcolm shook his head. "Sure, but why don't we just stay out here for a bit first. We can go back in later."

I backed up a few steps and took a deep breath. "How about I just go get you something and, you, stay right here."

I grabbed my own cup from the table and raced back to the door, my heart pounding against my ribs as if sending a Morse code message to my brain to get on the same track. *You can do this, Brea. Stop being such a scaredy-cat. It's just a kiss. People kissed all the time.* About twenty of them were kissing right now in various corners of the house. Except, it wasn't just a kiss, it was *the* kiss. The one I'd been wanting for so long. Is this how I wanted to remember it? Some random one-off?

In the kitchen, I snatched the closest red cup and filled it with the contents of a silver can from the cooler. Then I took a sip from my own drink, trying to slow the blood pounding against my temples. I needed to stop overthinking this. It could be simple. I quickly checked the faces in the room for Sasha. Where was she? What would she say if she were right here? She'd tell me to get out of my own head and calm down. She'd tell me to relax and let things happen. But, she'd also tell me to trust my instincts.

Taking a deep breath, I balanced the cups in my hands and slithered back through the crowd toward the deck door, trying to find words to explain what had just happened. Malcolm probably though I was a total freak. How would I be able to recover from that?

I struggled with the door handle but stopped, the drinks nearly tumbling to my feet.

Through the glass I saw Malcolm and some other girl twisted together like gnarled roots. All tongues, teeth, and hands, grabbing at my heart and shredding it into clumps of bloody muscle tissue. I stumbled back a step, beer sloshing over my hand. Who was she? Just a mass of dark hair under the moonlight—I couldn't tell anything else with Malcolm practically eating her face. He turned her toward the railing and pulled her closer as my stomach churned, my dinner threatening to make an encore appearance.

"See, I told you. That guy's kind of a dick."

I swirled around, thankful for the distraction and concentrating on not puking on the voice's shoes. Except, as I saw his face, I almost made an exception. Declan Noche. Just what I needed.

I walked away from the door, pushing him back into the room and away from the borderline NC-17 drama unfolding on the deck. After ditching the cups on the fireplace mantle, I rubbed my hands over my face, trying to compute what just happened.

"Did you come all the way here just to tell me how stupid I am? Because if you did, you wasted your time. I've figured it out myself."

He peeked around me toward the deck and grimaced, then stared down at the carpet. "No. I came here to wish you a happy birthday."

"Oh." The nausea came back for another gut-wrenching wave. I needed to start keeping my mouth shut. Except, maybe if I had, I'd be just another Malcolm Rogers statistic right now. Declan would do more than laugh if it were me out on that deck right now and, by Monday morning, Malcolm had moved on to the next girl. "Thank you. I thought you said you probably wouldn't come?"

More like now I wished he hadn't come. I really shouldn't care, but his words from earlier rang like alarm bells through my brain. *You deserve better.* Had he already known that Malcolm would jump at the first available lips? Or maybe somewhere beneath all the sarcasm and side eye he actually cared? My skin prickled, the odd tingle coming back, except this time I worried about what it meant.

"I did. But I changed my mind. Don't want you nagging me at my locker all year because I didn't show." A soft, uncharacteristic smile graced his lips. It suited him. He almost looked handsome when he wasn't trying so hard to be menacing.

My shoulders relaxed. "Good idea. I guess you've almost got me figured out."

"I didn't think I had a choice. But don't worry, I don't think I'll ever get you fully figured out. Too much work." Declan chuckled, but it turned into a cough and he tucked his mouth into his arm. "Sorry about that."

"Are you okay?"

Maybe it was the lights, or the fact that the room seemed to spin around us, but his eyes looked dull and sunken into his face. His lips also seemed to have lost their color, pale and bloodless against his skin.

"Yeah, just not feeling the best. But I'll be fine."

"Hey, D," a girl in a studded leather jacket called from behind him. "This sucks. Let's bounce."

Declan glanced over his shoulder. "Just a second."

Three clearly unimpressed party guests, two guys and the girl in the leather jacket, looked around the room as if they'd stepped out of a spaceship and landed on Planet Party with no travel guide. They dressed in the same I-hate-color style as Declan and, standing together, looked like they would've made an epic garage band, except I think they'd probably punch me in the face if I asked them to sing.

"Are those your friends?"

"Actually, they're more like family. We kinda get each other, you know?"

"Yeah. I do." Like me and Sasha. "Well, I wouldn't want you to leave your family waiting. Thanks for stopping by, though."

I mashed my fingers together in front of me, twisting them around as I became suddenly unsure of what to do with my hands. My mind still reeled at the humiliation of rejecting Malcolm in my crazy awkward way, and then getting rejected even worse right back. Declan glanced down and wrapped his palm over my nervous digits. His cool skin soothed my burning flesh, and he sighed as he leaned close to my ear. "Forget about Malcolm. I told you, you deserve better."

He threw me one last knowing grin then disappeared into the crowd, following his renegade crew toward the door. I watched him walk away, part of me aching for him to stay.

I blinked and snapped back to my senses. What was that? First Malcolm is the bad guy and now Declan is the good guy? The entire world had flipped upside down. I grabbed my drink from the mantle and took a big gulp, trying to wash down the mountain-sized lump that had grown in my throat. I checked my cell phone: 11:58.

Dammit.

If I kept Tori waiting, I'd never be able to leave the house again. I slammed back the rest of the cup and left it next to the untouched beer.

The heat of the crowd and the flash of embarrassment mixed and mingled in my blood and I started to sweat. Then, someone turned up the volume on the party, but the sound thickened as if I were listening from underwater. I pressed my fingers to my temples. Laughter boomed and cackled around me. Voices screamed and shouted. Above me. Below. Everywhere.

My foot stumbled and I grabbed onto the edge of the couch to keep from falling. I steadied myself, but the room kept moving. Light and color swirled around my head. I needed to leave. Streaks of red-lipped smiles floated past as I pushed myself closer to the front door. Acid burned the back of my throat. I jerked forward as I overstepped, and the light faded away. Pain stung my left foot. My right knee. My elbows. Then—*crack*—my head hit the floor. Shrieks echoed above me.

"Brea. Brea. Talk to me, Brea." Cold fingers brushed my face. Voices calling my name dropped out and disappeared one by one. My hands and feet vanished. I couldn't feel my body anymore. No light. No life. No thoughts. Just darkness.

5

———————

My head ached.

The vein running behind my left eye throbbed hard, threatening to force my entire eyeball out of its socket. I couldn't move. My arms and legs seemed frozen in place with sharp, stabbing pain surging through every nerve.

I struggled to open my eyelids. Still dark night, but all the stars had run away from the scarlet red sky. The horizon burned as if someone had set the heavens on fire. Maybe they had. The large harvest moon lost its magic against the blood-like sky. It now looked like a warning beacon, telling me to run.

Maybe the bizarre pain in my head meant I'd died and gone to Hell. Except the searing pain came from more than just my fall. Black, thorny brambles sprouted from the ground and twined around my legs, biceps, and wrists, pinning me to the foreign forest floor.

My pulse pounded in my ears and I struggled against the restraints, causing the razor-sharp thorns to slice stripes into my flesh. The more I struggled, the tighter the plants constricted.

How did I get here?

Images flashed through my brain. Sasha's party. Malcolm. Declan. Rushing to meet Tori. The world spinning as I fell. Then this. Whatever "this" was.

"Help," I screamed into the eerie night. "Is anyone out there?"

My breath shortened, each labored exhale piling up on the next and closing like a belt around my chest.

Footsteps, or maybe just the rustle of leaves, swirled around me.

"Please, help!" I screamed again.

No response, except for the hungry howl of an animal. It sounded like a wolf, but stronger, more feral, and far too close. I wrestled against the thorns as they clamped tighter into my skin. I dropped my mouth open and tossed my head back in a silent cry. Pain raged through my muscles. Tears poured down my face. I couldn't die here. Not tonight.

I curled my fingers toward my wrists to try and pull at the vines. They were just plants. They hurt, but they had to break. Just like in biology class. Everything could be dissected if you knew how. But my fingers couldn't reach them.

Starting with my left hand, I tried to slide out of the vines, but the restraint around my arm kept it locked in place. Only one way out now—through. I balled my hand into a fist and twisted, bending at the elbow and pulling straight up toward my shoulder. The thorns dug deep, and flashes of pain blurred in front of my eyes. I bit the side of my cheek to keep from screaming again and pulled harder.

Crack.

The vine snapped around my wrist and my hand broke free. The vine shimmied and flailed, as if alive, then regenerated from its torn end and swooped back toward my hand. I pressed my hand against my body, away from the vine. It missed its target and flopped back down to the ground.

What the hell? Since when did plants start growing back on their own?

The dangerous howl rang out again, even closer this time.

My heart pounded faster. No time for analysis. I needed out. Now.

I clenched my teeth and rolled toward my right side. The thorns ripped my flesh, and agony bubbled through me, my vision going black. I rolled through the pain until the rest of my arm swung free.

The vines moved and undulated, threatening to capture me again, but I stayed on my side, shielding my arm against my chest. The vines scratched at my back and I reached for a thick branch from a nearby bush. I yanked it, trying to pull myself free from the vines that still bound my legs and my other arm. The brittle branch gave way, breaking off in my hand and tossing me back to the ground.

I slid the broken end of the branch between the vines near my right wrist and pressed up, using the stick's leverage to pry the thorns away from my skin until I could pull my hand through. I did the same with the vines on my upper arm, this time with more difficulty.

The thorns carved crimson stripes through the sleeve of my dress and deep into my skin.

Sitting up, I set my legs free then scrambled away on my hands and knees. Dirt caked into my wounds, stinging my whole body. One vine caught my foot and dragged me backward. I wound up and kicked as hard as I could with my heel until it retreated with a strange hiss.

Once I was out of reach, the vines did a macabre dance, writhing and twisting in the air for its prey. I collapsed on my back, my heavy breath steaming from my mouth, then quickly thought better of it and limped to my feet. Where was I? The foreboding sky and the naked, bulbous trees looked nothing like the woods near Faraway. How did I get from Sasha's to this place? Was it even the same night? And the most frightening question of all—who would've brought me out here to die? I'd learned about carnivorous plants in science, but none that were big enough to attack a human being. And even if they were, this was Iowa. I'd expect to be attacked by ears of corn before a briar of thorns.

The sour, metallic smell of my own blood lingered in the air as I clutched my massacred arms closer to my body to slow the bleeding. I turned in a circle, looking for any type of landmark—a light or a path to lead me anywhere but here. Nothing. Just a dense fog rising from the dead forest floor and clouding the clearing. No way out.

My stomach churned and a dizziness overcast my brain as I stumbled around. What was happening to me? The pain and fear overwhelmed my senses. I dropped to my knees and retched, over and over, until all the badness wrung itself out. Tears soaked my cheeks. My arms shook as I crawled forward trying to get back onto my feet. I wanted to go home.

THE EERIE WOODS NEVER ENDED. Each desolate path connected to another, each one darker than the last. The trees twisted overhead like skeleton hands waiting to reach down and snatch me up. The terrifying howls continued, standing every hair of my body on end.

But the worst thing was the stares. I felt them. Sensed them. Tracing my movements as I fumbled through the forest. Sometimes I'd think I saw eyes following me like lasers in the denser clusters of trees. Sometimes they simply hung on my back like a heavy quilt, smothering and weighing me down.

Eventually, a small pond appeared in the middle of a thick stand of trees. I'd been walking . . . who knew how long? The moon never moved from its high point in the blood sky. Did time even exist here? Or did it run on an endless loop, one disastrous terror after another?

I collapsed near the water's edge. My throat begged for a drink, and my parched tongue seconded the idea. But should I dare? I scanned the woods one last time before I risked diverting my attention. Nothing out there but the stares.

I dipped my hand into the cool, crisp pond and drizzled the water onto my legs, scrubbing some of the dirt and dried blood from the cuts. My skin stung and I sucked air through my teeth to counter against the bite. I moved on to my wrists and arms, allowing the water to cleanse and refresh my aching limbs. Once I'd cleaned up, I stared at the water, wondering if I should risk a drink. I'd heard so many stories about travelers dying from polluted water. And who knew what kinds of things might live here?

I started with a taste, a small drop on my tongue. It seemed fine. Slightly salty, but drinkable. I took a little more and waited. Still okay. Then, I leaned over and took a large handful. My arm yanked forward, nearly pulling me into the pond. Webbed blue fingers clenched tightly on my wrist. I screamed and twisted my arm back and forth, trying to break the hold, but the fingers pulled harder. I leaned back, away from the water, and ripped my arm toward my chest. The grip released and I tumbled back onto the rocky ground.

I scrambled to my feet and ran without looking back.

The trees changed again. The moon stayed still.

My legs pushed onward but began to slow, each step harder to take than the last. Finally, I bent over and held my knees, panting hard in the dark. Tears formed and cascaded down my cheeks. What was happening to me? Where was I? What had I done to deserve this? My desperate gasps echoed on the breeze followed by another hungry howl in the dark. I wiped the back of my arm against my face. Not even time to be scared. Why was this happening?

I forced myself upright again and searched my surroundings. To the right, the woods seemed to thin as the crash of rolling waves came from that direction. Waves or thunder. Either way, something new. I put my hands on my hips and took a deep breath. Would the water lead me home? Could there be people on the other side of the woods? A town or a city that could help me figure out where I was?

A renewed hope charged in my veins. I took a step forward, but my body jerked back. An arm wrapped around my torso as fingers clamped down across my mouth. My body tensed, paralyzed, as a heavy breath fell on the back of my neck.

"When I let you go, you have to promise not to scream," a male voice whispered in my ear.

I gulped and nodded as best I could against the hand holding my head.

He relaxed his grip and I bolted forward, out of reach, before turning around. The eerie moonlight cast a strange glow across Declan Noche's grave expression.

"You!" I spat as I stepped backward, not willing to be any closer, but not letting him out of my sight.

He crept toward me. "What are you doing here? What happened to you?" He took my arm and reached to touch my wounds, but I ripped my hand out of his grasp.

"Man-eating vines, I think. Shredded me as I tried to escape. But I'm sure you already knew that."

He shook his head. "Why would I know that? Your cuts look really bad. Let me take a look."

"Oh, right. You don't know? I get dropped, alone and restrained in some weird alternate universe, and you just happen to be here." I tossed my hands in the air and yelled, "Why did you do this to me?"

His eyes widened, wild and dark, as he placed his index finger across his lips. "Keep your voice down. If you have any chance of surviving, you need to stop letting everyone know you're here."

I dropped my voice as demanded, but the rage pumping through me stayed at full blast. "What are you talking about? Who is 'everyone,' and where is 'here'?"

"You don't know?" Declan grabbed the back of his neck and started to pace in small circles in front of me. His thoughts flipped across his face like flashcards. "Then we're in a lot more trouble than I thought. How did you even get here?"

"Where. Is. Here?"

He tossed his head back and huffed as he rubbed the heels of his hands into his eye sockets. "You know when you were a kid and you thought there was a monster under the bed or in your closet? Or when you watched a scary movie with your friends and had nightmares for a week afterward?"

"Yeah."

He swept his arms open wide. "Welcome to the Midnight Realm. Home to every terrifying thing you've ever imagined, and probably ones your brain is even too scared to think of."

"And you brought me here?" I rushed at him, my finger pointing straight at his chest. "What's your problem? What did I ever do to you?"

This had to be some kind of prank. His friends thinking they were funny by pulling some stupid trick on me to see me squirm. These cuts were not a joke. My safety was not a joke.

"I had nothing to do with how you got here." He wrapped his hand around my wrist and pulled me toward him. His eyes glared down into mine, arguing his innocence since he couldn't shout it out loud. "I planned on getting the hell out the second I ended up in this wicked place, but I heard you calling for help and came looking. Now, keep your voice down before something less friendly decides to start hunting."

"Hunting?"

"Yes, hunting. Whoever got you into the Midnight Realm doesn't expect you to leave. The only thing I can't figure out is how a human could get in? Someone must have some powerful magic and a severe hate on for you in order to make that happen."

Tears welled in my eyes and I used the last of my strength to push them down. He wouldn't get the satisfaction of making me cry. "What did I do to make someone hate me this much?"

"I don't know. But for now, let's worry about getting you out of here."

"Right, like I should trust you? You might be leading me even farther into this disaster. I'll get out my own way."

He laughed and released my arm. "You won't last in here, Brea. It's more dangerous than you know."

"Then I guess you don't know me very well. I'm a lot stronger than I look. And don't ever tell me what I can and can't do." I charged past him, struggling to keep upright as I tripped and stumbled over the exposed roots and rotting branches on the forest floor.

He hurried after me, his voice low. "I'm not saying you can't, I'm saying you need help. There's a difference between strong and stubborn. Strong saves your life, stubborn gets you killed."

"I'll be fine. See you on the other side. If you make it."

He cut across my path. "Just let me help you."

I ducked around him, but he jumped back in my way again.

"Those eyes watching you. The ones you can feel weighing on the back of your skull, they are doing one of only two things: a) stalking you until they find the perfect moment of weakness, or b) waiting, because they know you're intended to be dinner for someone else. Someone a lot scarier than they are."

I shivered. I didn't want to meet them, let alone their boss.

"How come you know so much about this place?"

"It's a long story, but please let me help you find an exit." Declan swallowed, and his stare softened. "If I left you here and you didn't make it, I'd never forgive myself."

"Don't be—"

A mournful cry echoed through the trees. Declan's ear perked up like a cat's as he scanned the horizon. The cry moaned again. Louder. Sadder. My heart ached at the melancholy chords pumping heavy sorrow through my blood.

"What is that?" I asked.

"Keep moving." He linked his arm with mine, careful of the cuts, and led me onward. "It's a banshee. And that sound . . . it means someone is going to die."

6

———

"So, where do you think we should start?"

The wail moaned off in the distance and I tried to focus despite my shaking limbs. Declan straightened his posture, trying to look brave, except the childlike fear in his eyes betrayed him.

He marched to the right like a freight train ripping through a prairie. "I think we should head for the castle. If there's a portal anywhere, I'll bet it's there."

I thought his plan over in my brain then started walking left. "Wouldn't it make more sense to go back to the place I arrived? If there was a way in, then there should be a way out."

Declan stopped and turned around. "Did you see one while you were being attacked by man-eating vines? Or do you want to try to trust me for half a second."

I didn't. I didn't want to trust him at all. Trusting people only gave them more room to let me down. But, unfortunately, I did believe in logic, and if there was a castle in this godforsaken place, then someone that cared about having an actual house had to have lived here at some point. If they didn't have a portal, they might at least have some information.

"Fine. But when we get there and there's nothing, don't blame me."

Declan shook his head and kept walking. I followed behind, trying to get in front of him, but his legs were too long and his gait too determined to pull it off.

"You still haven't explained how you got here," I said, as we headed deeper into the dark forest.

The stares on my back weighed heavier in this direction. Either more creatures were watching from the woods or it was just the exhaustion of more walking.

"Like you, I wasn't expecting to come here. I just sort of showed up."

"But you weren't captured on arrival?"

"No. I just kind of slipped in. And until I found you, I'd planned on slipping out without being noticed."

A briny scent prickled my senses. Up ahead the trees thinned except for a few odd stands near a rocky shore. A large rolling field stretched out before us, leading to a gothic stone castle resting high on a peak, surrounded by the turbulent sea. Wind swelled off the rough waves that thundered against the shoreline.

Declan turned to me. The marine air blew dark strands of his hair over his eyes. "Almost there. How are you doing?"

"I'm good. Let's just get me home."

He nodded and kept moving. The tips of my fingers and toes froze in the cold openness but I trudged on, holding onto the warmth of hope that this might be over soon.

Behind us, a low rumble built. I picked up my pace. The sound increased with every step. Louder and louder. Closer and closer.

I threw my hands over my ears. "Declan, what is that?"

He looked up at the sky. Streams of black lines—crows—flew fast toward the castle.

"Oh no."

Declan grabbed my arm and started to drag me along. I glanced back as a dark cloud appeared, following the birds. Thick and dense shutting out the moon.

"Are those all crows?"

"No. It's the Sluagh. Run!" He dragged me behind him, my toes sometimes never touching earth as we whipped over the small hills of the field.

"What's the Sluagh?" I yelled over the noise.

"It's the evil dead. Souls so broken even the devil won't take them. If they catch you, they will take you with them for eternity."

The crows alit and covered the field like a uniformed first line. Behind them, human-sized creatures with leathery wings descended upon the field. Red eyes burned in skeleton-like faces with noses sunken in or completely missing. A strip of coarse fur like a mohawk bristled down their spines.

"Too late. Need to hide."

We raced to a large elm tree and cowered on the far side.

"They tend to travel west. If we can keep quiet, maybe they'll pass right by."

Declan wrapped himself around me, shielding me

between himself and the rough bark of the tree. The Sluagh moved lightning fast, traveling around us on their clawed feet, their winged arms oscillating around them. Hollow clucks echoed through the air as the beasts communicated with one another in a sound that emanated from deep inside their scaly chests.

"Shh," Declan whispered. The sound rolled over my cheek, feeling it before I heard it.

Our hearts thumped in double time, locking into a syncopated rhythm and threatening to expose us. Every muscle in my body clenched, the cuts in my skin searing again from the pressure of Declan's limbs over my own.

The clucks faded into the distance and Declan started to breathe again. He relaxed and edged away from the tree.

"Those things are horrible," I said, still staring off after them in the distance.

"Yeah, but it could have been worse."

He took a few steps away from the tree and held out his hand. "C'mon. Almost there."

I reached out. Declan's fingertips grazed mine as he flew sideways and crashed to the ground. A giant wing flapped. Red glowing eyes materialized in front of my face. The Sluagh.

I screamed and tried to move but it wrapped its translucent wing around the tree, trapping me in place. It's three-fingered claw clasped onto my shoulder, the middle talon double the size of the others. A dinosaur claw, yet more sinister.

"Declan!"

It pierced into my back. White hot pain seared my shoulder blade. My arm fell limp to my side. The Sluagh reared back its weathered bone head. Two lines of pointed canine teeth dripped green saliva. The rot of death and week-old garbage assaulted my nostrils. I bucked hard, slamming my knee into its bony torso again and again, each blow doing nothing—like hitting steel. I punched up, nailing its jaw. My fist exploded in torment, my knuckles hanging loose and likely broken.

Its hot breath drew closer and I closed my eyes, waiting to die. My pulse pounded like alarm bells in my brain, but I had nowhere to run. Maybe in death the pain would stop, or maybe I would just drag along in torture like this forever.

The Sluagh squealed, a high-pitched screech that perforated my eardrums. I opened my eyes. Declan wrapped his arm around the Sluagh's neck and pulled it backward. It retracted its claw and I wriggled from its grip as he wrestled it to the ground.

I stumbled back out of the terrible beast's reach. The Sluagh covered Declan with its veined wings, forgetting all about me.

Declan screamed. Over and over as the creature bit down on his shoulder. I had to do something.

I dragged myself closer, my limbs barely responding to me anymore. Red stained the ground behind Declan's shoulder. Each terrified shriek stabbed me in the chest. I pulled back my one good leg and kicked the back of the Sluagh's head at the base of its evil skull.

It pulled back, giving Declan room to move. He kicked high with his heavy boot, square in the middle of its chest. There was a sickening crunch and the Sluagh cowered, covering itself with its wings.

Declan pulled up off the ground and limped over to

my side. The two of us hobbled for the beach and collapsed on the shore. Behind us, the flap of wings intensified and the wounded Sluagh exploded into the air, following the rest of its vicious flock.

We lay on the ground. Bleeding. Panting. Broken.

Declan rested his forehead against mine, the weight of the battle bearing down on both of us. "Are you okay?"

"I think so."

We gasped for breath, our faces close together, our breath mingling, as if staying together kept us safe.

"I'm going to be in so much trouble over this." Declan's eyes drifted off, pain and fear dragging his focus. I placed my hand on his cheek, his skin burning against my palm.

"Thank you. I wouldn't have survived that without you."

"You did pretty good for a rookie."

Words about how I owed him my life, and how I'd make it up to him caught in my chest, held down for another time, but in this moment, I only had energy for one response.

I brushed my lips against his, waiting. He leaned into the kiss, his arm wrapping around my back and tugging me closer. His lips, much softer than I'd expected, moved with an urgency, as if kissing me kept him alive. Like water. Like oxygen.

A strange glowing pink light flashed between us. It grew brighter, and the pain evaporated from my body.

I closed my eyes, letting the pleasant sensations over-take the bad. His gentle fingers against my spine. The tip of his tongue tasting my lips. The soft airy gasp of breath between kisses.

Beep.

His hands released me and left a chill in their place.

Beep.

His heavy scent of cologne and sweat and blood vanished.

Beep.

Then his lips pulled away. I reached for them, but my lips fell on open air. Light appeared behind my eyelids. Bright and blinding.

I held my arm over my eyes to shield them, then dared to look around.

Beep. Beep. Beep.

Fluorescent lights and itchy low-grade cotton sheets scratched against my skin. I lowered my arm, the heart rate monitor attached to my finger beeping in the corner and drawing its perfect graphs of life. I'd made it. I'd escaped the Midnight Realm. But where was I now?

7

———————

J hated hospitals. Maybe because I'd never really spent much time in one, or maybe because any time I did came with bad news. I rubbed my hands over my face and scanned the stark room. Today, unfortunately, I didn't know if lying in this lumpy bed was good or bad. A sudden memory of thorns and claws flashed in my mind and I inspected my arms. No cuts or blood. Not even a scratch on my thighs. I tossed the sheets back and swung my legs over the side of the bed.

"Don't even think about it, child."

Margaret Danley, Faraway's own Mother Teresa, sat in the corner, not even looking up from her crochet to reprimand me. Typically, we'd only spoken at the Twisted Top or during the Christmas hamper drive, but Aunt Becky always raved about how she wanted to be just like her when she became an old woman. Kind. Humble. Selfless. But why would she be hanging out with me? I looked at the blipping heart monitor near my bed. Could she be an angel or something? Maybe this hospital scene was fake and I'd actually died?

"What are you doing here? Where's my aunt?" I blurted as the peaks on the heart line sped up and spiked higher on the screen.

She tugged off her reading glasses and poked them into her white hair, then finally turned to acknowledge me. I tried not to stare at the white spots on her left eye. They seemed to be getting worse. For all the good Mrs. Danley did for the community, you'd think someone somewhere would grant her mercy. Wouldn't she be healed if she were an angel?

"I came to deliver some donated toys to the children's wing when I ran into Tori, so I sent her and her belle to have some lunch. Poor Rebecca. Sitting vigil so long wears on the soul. I practically had to drag her out of this chair." She chuckled and tucked her ball of yarn into a large straw bag sitting by her feet.

Aunt Becky was here. The heart monitor slowed again as my shoulders fell back down. "How long have I been asleep?"

"Well, they hauled you in here Friday night, so that would make it about three days or so."

"Three days? How could I be asleep for three days?"

"Don't ask me, dear. I just came into the story, remember?" She pushed up slowly from the chair, her arms shaking as they supported her. She shuffled over to my side and bunched the covers in her fist.

"Now, why don't you just lie back and get some rest. Your aunt will be back in a few minutes, but I don't want you to hurt yourself in the meantime."

I opened my mouth to argue, but a wave of vertigo

washed over me and I decided not to fight. "All right. I'm not sleeping though. I had the weirdest dream."

She turned her head, giving me a creepy side eye. "Interesting. Sometimes dreams are trying to tell us something about our reality."

She tucked the hem of the blanket under my chin and smoothed the hair off my forehead. Her wrinkled skin brushed soft like kitten fur against mine.

"I doubt this one was. If so, there's some pretty weird stuff going on in this town."

"You'd be surprised." She laughed. "Rest now."

"I hear what you're saying, Tori, but I'm not sure if it's the right time—" Aunt Becky appeared in the doorway. She glanced over at me and I forced a smile. Her eyes blasted wide and she ran toward me. Tori reached around and grabbed her coffee from her hand before the paper cup went flying.

"Brea. You're awake. You're okay." Tears flowed fast and hard down her cheeks, making dark polka dots on her light blue T-shirt. She lay down across the bed with me and held tight to my shoulders in an awkward hug. I tilted my head toward hers and wrapped my fingers around her arm, clenching tight, her soft hair tickling my chin.

"Well, I guess I should be going. Pleased to see that all is well." Mrs. Danley pulled on her coat and headed out the door with her straw bag, nodding at Tori as she moved into the hall. "But, Miss Breanne, if you ever need to talk about those dreams, you know where I live."

"What was that about?" Tori asked after the old woman had rounded the corner.

"Nothing. I don't really want to talk about it."

She shrugged and came to the side of the bed, gripping the metal railing beside me.

"How are you feeling?" Aunt Becky asked, allowing me a small fraction of room to breathe.

"A little dizzy." My stomach gurgled from beneath the sheets, loud enough that all three of us stared. "And pretty hungry."

"Hungry? Hungry's good. I'll go talk to the doctor and see what they can get you," Tori said. She put down Aunt Becky's coffee cup on the small wheeled table near my head, then disappeared off to the nurse's station.

Aunt Becky and I sat in silence for a few minutes, hanging onto each other as if one of us might slip away. I'd missed her so much. I hadn't even realized the extent until I smelled her shampoo and it transported me back home. Where I was safe. Eventually, the question burning in my brain finally settled down into my throat. "So, what happened?"

At that she sat up and ran her fingers through my hair. Her tears had slowed but they kept pooling, and her forehead wrinkled with concern all the way down to around her eyes. "What do you remember?"

I closed my eyes for second. The bodies of everyone at the party around me. The moonlight cutting through the windows. The taste of watermelon. The scent of sweat. "I remember trying to leave the party, then everything started spinning."

"The doctors say you were poisoned. They found traces of nightshade in your system."

"Nightshade? What's that?"

"It's a plant. Dark berries and poisonous leaves. Did you go out for a walk in the woods or anything?"

I closed my eyes. I never wanted to walk in the woods again. After that crazy dream, I would never look at trees the same. "I don't think so."

"Then it must've been in something you ate or drank. I knew I shouldn't have let you go."

Poisoned. Could it really be true? I barely had anything all night except the one drink I started with. Would someone really be so evil as to slip something in there?

"Did anyone else end up in the hospital?"

She shook her head and cupped her palm on my cheek. "Once you passed out, the police came and broke up the party. If anything else happened, I haven't heard about it."

Sasha must be so mad. I definitely knew how to ruin a party.

"Can I go home soon?"

"We'll have to see. The doctor may want to keep you for observation a little while longer."

Tori appeared in the doorway. "Good news. They'll be right up with some lunch."

"Thanks," Aunt Becky said. "Now, Brea, just lie back and get some rest. Your body's been through a lot the last few days, and the quicker you get better, the quicker we can get you out of here and bring you home."

I wriggled around, trying to find a comfortable spot and failing. I closed my eyes, feeling Aunt Becky's fingertips floating over my face. Then the room went dark. The dead trees flashed above me. The crows. The thorns.

I whipped my eyes back open. "I'm not really that tired right now."

8

Aunt Becky flung open the door. Lavender essential oils. Pungent lemon disinfectant cleaner. Then that one thing, the one scent that hung over everything and smelled like everything and nothing at all—the home smell. No matter where I went or how long I'd been gone, it would always be home the second I got a hint of that smell. Plus, a little something strange clouded over it all. Chow mein maybe?

I pulled myself into the house. Aunt Becky tried to help, but I shrugged her off.

"You're back." Tori met us at the door, clapping her hands. "I know it's not as great as Becks' cooking, but I sprang for the deluxe meal from Double Rainbow. If you don't want Chinese, that's cool. I can always go to Fat Tony's or Misty's or wherever it is you want."

I chuckled. Tori's excitement bled into my aching body and gave me more strength than any of the medicine the doctors had put in me. "Chinese sounds great. Anything will be better than hospital food."

I collapsed in my regular chair as Aunt Becky gave Tori a peck on the cheek and helped her stick serving spoons into the aluminum takeout containers. The sticky sweet and sour, honey garlic, and a hint of hoisin made my mouth water. I wiped my arm across my mouth and tried to stay polite until Tori and Aunt Becky at least sat down. I didn't realize that being asleep for three days would give me thirty days of hunger.

Aunt Becky smiled. "Help yourself, Br—"

I didn't wait for her to finish or even dwell on the fact that I must have looked like a mangy runaway dog or something. I just started loading up my plate, popping a chicken ball in my mouth to give me energy for this simple chore.

I chomped down on a spring roll, the flaky shell floating in my mouth with the most pleasant feeling. Except, I seemed to be the only one eating. Aunt Becky and Tori stood by the counter, their voices low. Aunt Becky crossed her arms over her chest, a pained crinkle to her forehead as she cast her eyes to the floor. Tori rubbed her shoulder and then tugged her into a hug, tracing her spine with her knuckles.

My fork hovered above my plate as I watched the unknown drama unfold. "Are you guys going to tell me what's going on?"

They let go of each other. Tori attempted to paint over her guilt with a beaming smile while Aunt Becky ran the back of her finger across her eyelashes and stood up straighter.

"It's nothing," she said. "Don't worry about it."

They both joined me at the table, their movements stiff and robotic.

"Are you sure? Did the doctor say something to you?" My breath started coming in shorter gasps. "Is there something wrong with me?"

Aunt Becky placed her hand on my arm. "No, you'll be just fine. They're actually shocked at how well you're doing."

"Good." My breathing returned to normal, and I shifted my focus back to my plate. The three of us ate in near silence, except for the clanging of forks against porcelain and the deep sighs of satisfied swallows.

"Did you want the last shrimp?" Tori held a container out in front of me. I nodded and spooned it onto my plate. "I'm glad you got your appetite back. I picked up a bunch of snacks at the grocery store. I'll be home early tomorrow, but I wouldn't want you to go hungry while we're at work."

"Thanks. But I'll be at school tomorrow, so it's no big deal."

Tori stared at Aunt Becky and shrugged.

Aunt Becky patted my hand. "I don't think that's the best idea. Maybe you should spend a few more days resting before you worry about that."

"Why? You already said they're surprised at how well I'm doing, and honestly, I feel great." I jumped up from the chair. A slight wave of dizziness rushed over me, but I smiled to cover it. "Besides, I wouldn't want to get behind on any of my work."

"I've already called the principal. I can pick up a package of your homework tomorrow and you won't miss a thing."

"But I want to go back to school. I'll be so bored here.

Plus, wouldn't it be better if I was around other people instead of here alone?"

Alone.

The empty corners of the silent house already haunted me. More time to remember the Midnight Realm and the other things I would rather forget. Even for a dream, it felt too real. Too visceral.

"But, are you sure you want to go back so soon after what happened? Everyone there will know. And possibly, someone there might've . . ." Aunt Becky's eyes filled with tears.

"Someone there might've been the one who poisoned me?"

She slammed her fist down on the table. "Doesn't that scare you? That anyone out there could've tried to hurt you? Someone sitting next to you in class, or standing behind you in the cafeteria line. It's not safe to leave yourself open like that."

"But, Aunt Becky, how do you even know that someone tried to hurt me? Maybe it was an accident? Or maybe whoever did it wasn't targeting me, or just picked someone at random. No matter what I do, no matter where I go, there will always be danger. I could walk out of the house and get hit by a bus tomorrow. Unless you expect me to stay inside forever, I'll never be completely safe."

"Then maybe that's what we should do. You're almost finished school anyway. Maybe we can figure something out for credits and you could homeschool for the next two years."

"Are you serious? I'm not going to be homeschooled when I'm trying to get into Princeton. You're being ridiculous." I stood up behind her and wrapped my arms around her neck, resting my chin on her head. "I know you're scared. I'm terrified. But locking me away isn't going to solve anything. Hiding will only tell whoever did this that they won. And if someone did this on purpose, the last thing I want is for them to feel victory."

She cringed in my arms and tucked her cold fingers around my wrist.

"Besides, if someone was intentionally trying to hurt me, keeping me at home would only tell them exactly where I was. At least if I try to live my life, I'd be a moving target."

"Please do not refer to yourself as a target."

"Fine. But you know what I mean. There are so many things to be afraid of in this world. Running from them won't make them go away."

"We could move." She pried my arms off her shoulders and started to pick up the empty takeout containers. "Tori, you've always wanted to live by the beach. Maybe we could head out to Florida or one of the Carolinas or something."

"As if that would be safer, Aunt Becky. We live in Iowa. If anything bad is going to get us in Iowa, it can get us anywhere."

"But maybe it could buy us a little time."

"You're being ridiculous. I'm going to school tomorrow. If there are any problems, I'll give you a call."

She narrowed her eyes at me, but I straightened my stance and popped my hands on my hips, staring right back. She had a point, but so did I.

Tori slid from her chair and rushed across the

kitchen to the paper bags on the counter. "Almost forgot. Can't have Chinese without fortune cookies."

She stepped between us, breaking our locked stares, and held out three fortune cookies in her palms. She nudged them toward Aunt Becky, who softened and took the one on the right. She offered them to me, and I pondered for a second before taking the one farthest away.

"See, isn't that better?" Tori grabbed her own cookie and squeezed it in her hand. The cellophane made a *pop* as it opened, and the cookie crushed in her fist. She teased out the small slip of paper.

"'A dream you have will come true.' Well that's positive, although super vague." She laughed and knocked at Aunt Becky with her shoulder.

Aunt Becky rolled her eyes but forced opened the plastic and uncovered her own fortune. "'You are very talented in many ways.'"

"Yes, you are." Tori gave her a soft kiss and she smiled. "At least one of us got a good one. What about you, Brea?"

I cracked the cookie open, the processed pastry crumbling in my hands. I pinched the piece of paper in my fingers and read the words. A chill ran down my back. "Uh . . . 'Your smile has the light of a thousand suns.'"

"That one's pretty good too," Tori said.

The three of us waltzed around the kitchen, clearing dishes and cleaning up without speaking or touching. As I scraped the few stray chow mein noodles from my plate into the garbage can, I tossed in the broken bits of fortune cookie. I pulled the paper out of my pocket and read the real fortune one more time before tossing it into the trash.

Be careful who you trust.

AFTER HOURS of trying to act okay, without making it obvious that I had to try, Aunt Becky finally relented and agreed to let me go to school. Anyone I knew would've begged to get out of class, yet I pleaded to go back. Someone should've questioned that.

I flipped the light on in my room and scanned every corner before entering. I may have convinced Aunt Becky that the whole incident wasn't targeted at me, but I didn't know for sure. I quietly slipped the door closed as the roar of the television downstairs confirmed that at least someone would be awake for a while if I needed them.

I crept over to the window and leaned my elbows on the frame. The stars twinkled bright in the sky as the moon glazed the street in blue light, almost like a river winding between the houses and the trees. The night painted a beautiful picture on the silent canvas of our boring little street, but instead of inspiring calm, I searched every shadow for a face, or maybe something darker, something sinister, lurking out there and staring back up at me. I ripped my arms from the window and backed up a step. My heart pounded faster. I forced a deep breath in through my nose and out through my mouth, except refusing to close my eyes.

One breath. Two breaths. Three deep breaths.

I released my fingers, which had unconsciously clenched into fists at my sides, and shook out the rest of the tension from my body. The daytime paranoia faded quickly, but the night still slithered wicked and murky through my bones. I forced myself to happier thoughts. Summer days by the lake, all-night chat sessions with Sasha when we should have been sleeping, trips to the city with Tori and Aunt Becky, Declan's lips pressed against mine . . . Wait . . . No, no, no. I shouldn't think about that. He'd said he wasn't the one to bring me to the Midnight Realm, but how come he was the only one that had shown up there? Or was it really just a dream? Had I imagined myself in his arms?

But, could I really have dreamed up the salty taste of his lips, or the warmth of his breath on my cheek?

My hand slid up to my lips, the lingering memory of the kiss that may or may not have happened tingling across my skin. One more thing I needed to face tomorrow—the fact that it may have really happened. Or, even worse, that my subconscious wished it did.

I switched on the lamp beside my bed and pulled back the covers. Just my own bed, nothing to worry about. I flipped off the overhead light and lay down, yanking the navy comforter high enough that I could stare at the silver constellation pattern in the fabric without lifting my head.

The lamplight carved shapes on the ceiling and the walls, shadows looming off in the corners. My pulse spiked again.

One breath. Two breaths. Three deep breaths.

No relief. I tossed back the covers and raced to the door, flipping the lights back on then retreating to my bed. I pulled my knees to my chest and leaned against the headboard, staring straight at my bookshelf and the rainbow of book spines on each row.

For once I wished for the sedatives the doctor had given me in the hospital. They dried my mouth and fogged my brain, but at least I'd been able to close my eyes and fade into nothingness for a few hours. Now when I closed my eyes, I just saw that place. Lost souls and desperate creatures. Red eyes and varying shades of death.

I rocked forward and back against the headboard, wide awake, and created a mental list of suspects of potential poisoners. Whoever they were stole my sleep from me, and I would never let them forget it.

9

----

*D*eclan didn't show up.

I lingered by my locker, rearranging books and papers for forever, even waiting until after the bell to head to class. A three-day coma definitely did work on teacher sympathy though. As I waltzed into class late, probably for the first time ever, Mr. Sebastian didn't even flinch.

Then it was already lunchtime, my brain still foggy, not having heard a word anyone had said all morning. I swung back by my locker and dropped off my books, still on the lookout for Declan, but he never showed. My stomach growled and I splayed my hand over top of my shirt. At least one part of my body still seemed to be working fine. I adjusted my bag strap on my shoulder and weaved through the mass of Faraway students. For the first time, everyone looked at me. Not in the obligatory way like when I won an award or something, but a true center of attention. Some eyes squinted with sympathy, others with curiosity, and some—I cringed—

with pity. Except, the more they stared, the more I stared back, scanning every face, questioning if they may have been the one to hurt me.

My new nickname, the super original "Coma Girl," rippled in whispers through the cafeteria line. A hushed breeze of infamy weaving through the Jell-O cups and ham sandwiches. I shuffled my items onto the tray—iced tea, side salad, and a slice of pizza—concentrating on every movement as a way to block out the rest of the noise. Someone tapped my shoulder and I jumped, dropping my fork on the cheap linoleum floor. It clanged and drew more attention. The guy behind me who'd tapped, Austin Breckenridge from my English class, scooped it up and handed it back.

"Sorry, I didn't mean to scare you."

"It's fine. Just a little tired today, that's all."

He nodded, then looked back at his buddies behind him in line. "Hey, Brea, so we heard you actually died for like five minutes. Is that true?"

"No. If I'd died for that long I probably wouldn't even be out of the hospital yet." It came out sharper than I intended, but my tolerance ran low for pointless questions. "Were you even there? Did you come to the party and watch me fall and get carried away by an ambulance?"

His eyes bulged, but he suddenly couldn't look at me. "No. I wasn't there. It's just what everyone is saying."

"So, you didn't see anything. You have no idea what happened. You weren't there, but you seem to think that you know about it because someone told you something stupid?"

"I . . . uh . . ." He pried his buddies for support, but they abandoned him, looking off into the distance.

"Excuse my friend. She's had a rough week." Sasha appeared beside me and draped her arm over my shoulder, then clamped tight and steered me away from Austin. She jerked her head at Ainsley and Cora standing behind her. Ainsley took my tray and the two of them followed us to an empty table near the windows.

I slumped into the bench seat, the afternoon sun warming my back and adding kindling to the fire burning in my cheeks.

Sasha sat down beside me. "What was that all about? You seemed fine this morning. Now you're seconds from rolling some guy in the cafeteria?"

"I wouldn't have done anything." At least I didn't think I would've. "I guess I'm still a little tired and it's making me kinda grouchy."

"Tired? Didn't you sleep for like three whole days?" Cora shook her orange juice and laughed. I scoffed and rolled my eyes. She stopped shaking and put the container down.

"Okay. Too soon, huh?"

Sasha nodded. I pushed my tray away from me, then crossed my arms on the table and rested my head.

"I'm sorry, Brea," Cora continued. "I'm not trying to be rude. It's just that no one around here has met anyone who's been in a coma before. What was it like? Do you remember anything?"

I dared to close my eyes. The blood-red sky. The demonic faces of the Sluagh coming for me. I ripped my eyes open again and sat up straight. "No. I don't remember a thing."

Cora's shoulders slumped in disappointment, but she dropped the subject and moved on to her lunch.

"I'm sure it's better that way," Sasha said as she rubbed her hand down my back. "And again, I'm so sorry this happened to you at your own party. Some people are just depraved. But the police told my parents that, without proof, they probably won't be able to figure out who did it. They also said, depending on what was in your cup, it might have just been an accident."

"Maybe. But I'm not so sure about that."

"Why?" Ainsley asked. "Do you think someone would intentionally try to hurt you?"

"I'm not sure." I pulled out my calculus notebook and flipped toward the pages at the back, then laid it out on the table. "I made a list of everyone I remembered seeing at the party that night. Each one is highlighted based on how much interaction I had with them. Green means I saw them but we didn't speak or were never in close proximity. Yellow means they were around but not directly. And pink means they were someone I spent time with or was close to."

"Your list looks a lot different than mine would. I'd have way more pink." Ainsley laughed and ran her finger along the page down the list of names.

"If you guys notice anyone that I'm missing, I'll add them to the bottom."

"Nice. The three of us are the first ones listed." Cora pointed to the large blob of pink at the top of the page.

"I included everyone. I figured it would be the best way to make sure I didn't miss anyone."

"Look at you, party girl. Bright pink on Malcolm Rogers. What happened there?" Ainsley leaned on her elbows across the table.

"Nothing at all."

"I'll say. The next person on the list is 'Random girl making out with Malcolm.' Ouch!" Cora noted.

"Yeah. Didn't quite work out the way I'd hoped, but it's fine. And, unfortunately, I didn't really see who he was with. I just kinda looked away and blocked the whole thing out."

Sasha grabbed the book and looked it over, then tucked the cover under the bottom and pointed at the last name on the list. "Declan Noche. If anyone looks suspicious, it would be him. I remember seeing him leave just before you fell, and he is always looking at you funny when you are at your locker."

"What do you mean, 'funny'?"

"I don't know, like uncomfortable. Like he desperately needs to talk to you, but then doesn't. He's either rocking the stalker vibe or the boy is just thirsty and has no idea what to do about it."

I shivered. Maybe my subconscious did know more than I thought. "Possibly. I will definitely be checking him out—I mean . . . checking into him."

Sasha closed the book and held it up in front of me. "What exactly do you plan to do, B? You can't exactly investigate every single person that came to the party. And even if you did, what would you even do about it? If the police have zero leads, why do you expect that you would do any better?"

"I just need to know." I grabbed the notebook and pulled, but Sasha held tight, tugging it back.

"Seriously, though. Haven't you been through enough? Maybe you should just let this go and try to get back to your normal life. If there is anything I know about you it's how obsessive you can be about things, and I don't want to see you hurt yourself even more."

I pulled harder on the book and wobbled back on the bench as it released from Sasha's grip. "I'll be careful. I promise."

Sasha eyed me up and down, not believing a single word but knowing she didn't have a choice except to let me do my thing.

Ainsley grabbed her tray and stood, straddling the bench. "I'm going for a walk before class so I don't fall asleep in biology. Anyone wanna join me?"

"Yeah, sure." Sasha grabbed her things and followed. "You should come, Brea. Fresh air would probably do you some good."

"I'm fine. I'm going to go see if I missed any assignments from the beginning of the week. Go ahead."

Sasha frowned but obeyed, joining Ainsley as they strolled toward the exit. "Are you coming, Cora?"

"Just a minute." Cora glanced at them, then me, then down at her tray as she spun her fork over and over in her fingers. "I think you're doing the right thing trying to find out who might've poisoned you. If it was me, I'd want to know."

"Thanks, Cora. Everyone else probably thinks I'm insane."

"No one around here pays enough attention to us to care. Not really. By next week, no one will remember any of this happened."

I nodded. She had a point. Except I would remember, and that mattered to me.

Cora scooped her dark curls up in a ponytail then slipped the elastic band from around her wrist to tie them in place. She got up from the table with her tray. "I'll bet whoever it was is someone a lot closer to you than you think."

She turned and rushed after Ainsley and Sasha.

I pulled the notebook back out from my bag and scanned the list of names again. It could've been anyone. I sighed. Or maybe Sasha was right and it was all a mistake. A tragic accident.

The sun streaming through the window blared hotter, and my back started to get sticky from sweat. I yanked off my sweater and tucked it into my bag, then stopped. Two black marks stretched across the back of my wrist. I licked my thumb and rubbed it over my skin, but the marks didn't smudge.

Leaving my tray on the table, I grabbed my bag and ran out of the cafeteria to the bathroom down the hall. I turned on the tap and let the water run for a few seconds before plunging my hands underneath the stream. I scrubbed my wrist with my other hand, but the mark didn't come off. Two triangular black points stained like permanent ink or a tattoo across my skin. I hadn't even used markers today. The skin around the marks changed to red as I rubbed it raw, but it only made the marks darker. I finally turned the water off and looked in the mirror. Red spiderwebs had started spinning in my eyes from lack of sleep, matching nicely with the dark circles blossoming underneath them. I'd probably just been careless or something. Why was I panicking about—

Then I glanced at my shoulder reflected back in the mirror. A thick black line weaved down toward my arm with several triangular points sticking out from all angles. I clamped my hand over top of the mark, then traced the line with my finger. My stomach hollowed. I'd seen this shape before. In the Midnight Realm.

Thorns.

10

I ran my pen along the list of names in my notebook as I sat in the student lounge watching the few people who passed by in the hall. Most of the yellow names seemed squeaky clean. I'd asked around about them, searched their social media, and generally had no reason to keep them on the list.

The more I worked this, the more I seemed to be going in circles. Daytime meant looking for answers, but at night I hid, in case the answers came for me. Nothing seemed to make sense. If it was an accident, how did I end up in that horrible place? If that place was really a dream, why did I have a thorn bush growing out of my arm? Or had I just started hallucinating after two full nights of not sleeping? But what else was I supposed to do?

The class bell rang and the hall started to fill up again. I had a quiz in calculus, but for once I hadn't even studied. My mind was too consumed with everything else. Plus, when I tried to concentrate on the numbers, they kind of blurred and fell out of order. I needed to get control back in my life, but I couldn't do that until I knew what happened, a vicious circle leaving me to spin and spin and spin.

I chucked my notebook in my bag and rushed into the hallway, trying to make sure I was at least on time for the class I wasn't prepared for.

A dark patch of black-clad bodies appeared up ahead near Declan's locker.

Finally.

I picked up my feet and weaved through the crowded hallway as quickly as I could. Maybe it was a coincidence that he hadn't been here the day I came back. Or maybe not. He looked pretty sick at the party Friday night. Either way, he hadn't been crossed off my list of suspects yet.

Declan's friends huddled around him like bodyguards to a popstar, but unless he'd gone viral in the last few days, I doubted that was the case. They seemed to be the same three from the party—the bored girl, having traded her party leather for a dark hoodie, black jeggings, and surprising peacock blue nail polish, plus the other two Declan-styled twins who cast me odd glances as I bounded toward them.

"Hey, Declan, can I talk to you for minute?"

He spun around and shuddered, nearly falling back against the locker bank, but rebounded quickly—if I'd really seen anything at all. Maybe I'd just caught him off guard. Except for the odd moment of surprise, he seemed to have recovered. His cheeks were back to their full color, even if his wardrobe wasn't, and his lips had regained their deep red tone. His soft, full lips . . .

I shook my head. *Just a dream, Brea. Just a dream.* Plus, what if he was the one who'd tried to kill me? I was so messed up.

"Actually, I'm busy."

I leaned closer and lowered my voice. "Oh. Is it your army boot convention?"

His friends glared at me. He remained stone-faced. No chuckle. No sneer. Nothing.

"Yeah, and we're late." He jerked his head down the hallway, his entourage following close behind him, snickering at me as they passed.

"Are you gonna be back?" I yelled after him.

He didn't turn around.

I dialed in my combination and slammed my locker door open with a bang. Since when did he get all uptight? Did I insult him in front of his friends or something? No, wait. His "family." Seriously?

"What was that about?" Sasha appeared beside me, her long curly hair tied up in a bun with a few pretty strands loose around her face and neck.

"Nothing. Just getting a little frustrated, and still really tired."

"What are you frustrated about? I just saw you talking to that Declan guy. Did he say something to you? I told you he seems awfully suspicious."

"No. He was no help at all."

I pressed my forehead on the side of my locker and closed my eyes. The momentary rest relaxed my body, but the noises of the crowded hall kept me out of my own debilitating thoughts. Sasha rubbed my arm through my sweater and I flinched, as if she could see through the wool to my half-drawn mystical tattoo.

None of this made any sense. Why couldn't I figure this out?

"Brea, are you sure you're okay? You seem super off since you came back from the hospital. I know this is a pretty dramatic thing to go through. Maybe you need to take some more time to heal before trying to come back full-time."

"I said I'm fine," I snapped, then cringed at my tone. The lack of sleep made me irritable, but what would happen if I told anyone? They would think I was insane. They'd probably lock me up, or medicate me. It would be on my permanent record. I'd never be able to live it down.

Sasha ripped her hand away. "Then if you're fine, you need to get yourself together. I will be more than happy to help you with anything you need, but I can only do that if you tell me what's going on."

"I almost died, Sasha, and no one seems to be worried about who or what could still be out there."

She clutched my shoulders and maneuvered me in front of her, staring into my face and refusing to let me look away. "Of course I'm concerned, but I know you, and I know how obsessive you can get when you want to know something. You just need to take a step back and let this go. The police are looking into it. This isn't healthy for you."

I narrowed my eyes. "Why is it that you seem so hell-bent on making me drop this?"

She tossed her hands in the air. "You didn't just say what I thought you said, right?" She pointed her finger in my face and cocked her head to the side. "You didn't just accuse me of trying to poison you?

You're my best friend. Why would I do something like that?"

"No." I shook my head. "That's not what I meant."

Maybe it was?

"Well, good, because I wouldn't be taking that from anyone. Not even you." She wrapped her arm around me and squeezed. "You need to trust me on this. You never let anyone in unless they claw their way there. Look at these nails." She held up her black sparkly manicure. "I'm not going anywhere, unless you make me."

I rested my head on her shoulder, letting her vanilla scent lull me into a state of calm. "Okay. I'll try."

"Good." She nodded. "Now, we were all going to head to Fat Tony's tonight to hang out, but if you aren't feeling up to it, we can totally cancel and I can just come to your place and chill. Or you can get some of that sleep you so desperately seem to be needing."

"No. Fat Tony's sounds great."

The bell rang for the next class and Sasha stiffened next to me. "Okay, gotta go, but I'll see you there later."

Sasha rushed down the hall toward her class. I grabbed my calculus textbook and closed the locker door. Was she really that concerned about me, or was she hiding something too?

11

The television blared in the corner as I read my calculus homework again. The numbers jumbled around on the page. Paying attention on minimal sleep already presented a challenge, but the droning voices and laugh track made it nearly impossible. I covered my ears, unable to concentrate with the noise, but I couldn't bring myself to turn the show off and risk silence in the house. The moment I walked through the door now, I needed something. Music on my phone. The TV. One time I even sang to myself to fill the void.

The side door creaked open and I stood from the couch, peering into the kitchen.

"Who's there?"

"Just me." Aunt Becky appeared near the stove with a bag of groceries in her hand.

I slammed the textbook closed and walked out to meet her. She hoisted the bag onto the counter and I pulled out the sticks of celery and head of lettuce for the fridge.

"Thanks. I could've handled it though."

"I know. No big deal."

Aunt Becky closed her eyes and winced.

I stopped puttering with the food and stared at her. "Are you okay?"

She rubbed her temples and ripped her hair down from the French twist clinging to the back of her head. "Just a little headache. But I should ask you the same question. How are you feeling?" She ran the tap, fluttering her fingers under the running water, waiting for it to cool off.

"I'm good. Just trying to get some homework done."

She grabbed the Tylenol from the cupboard and filled a glass of water before swallowing it down with the medicine.

"Glad to hear. I still think you should have taken a few days at home, though."

"Maybe. But I'm doing okay. I wouldn't want to miss too much work anyway."

She gripped her neck with both hands and stretched her head back, letting out a small groan. "Any requests for dinner tonight?"

"Actually, I'm heading to Fat Tony's in about an hour. Don't worry about me."

She winced as her head dropped again. "I don't think that's a good idea. You should probably stay home tonight. Take it easy."

"Why? I go to Fat Tony's all the time. Besides, you know who I'll be with. Why shouldn't I go?"

She paused as if she had an argument, but decided to

choke it down instead. "I guess so. I just don't like you putting yourself in dangerous situations."

I laughed. "The only dangerous situation at Fat Tony's is if I overindulge on breadsticks and can't walk home."

"I'm not sure I like the idea of you walking by yourself either."

"Seriously, Aunt Becky. You need to lighten up. You can't just lock me down in this house."

She grabbed ahold of the counter, her knuckles flashing white as she gripped harder. "I know that. I just think, for the next little while, you should be more careful."

"Why? What's so important about right now?"

"Nothing. I just mean . . . since you've been in the hospital you're weaker, and you might become a target."

I gave her a hug. "You worry too much. You know that?"

"It's what I do. When you love someone as much as I love you, you'll do anything to keep them safe, even if it does seem a little much."

"And I want to see you safe as well, so go upstairs and lie down before that head gets any worse. I can bring you some tea."

Her shoulders relaxed at the suggestion. "That would be wonderful. You're a good kid, Brea. Don't ever forget that, okay?"

"And you need to go to bed. Scoot." I pressed my fingers into her shoulders and pushed her out of the kitchen. She reluctantly obeyed, and I searched the cupboard for the boxes of herbal tea.

I filled the kettle and plugged it in, then opened the

teabag and laid it in Aunt Becky's favorite "I hate Mondays" coffee mug. The sweet scent of pomegranate and hibiscus tickled my nose. I folded up the grocery bag and tucked it in the closet. As I closed the door, Aunt Becky's phone buzzed on the counter. I glanced over at the screen.

Daniel: We need to talk. ASAP.

I switched off the phone. Whoever it was could wait. Aunt Becky had always been good to me, and right now I need to take care of her.

12

The heavy smell of garlic and tomato sauce mixed with a little too much olive oil wafted out into the street, spreading nearly a block in every direction of the restaurant. A delicious lure to reel in business, except it wasn't like they needed it. Fat Tony's was the place to be any night of the week unless there was a party or a football game. Even then, most people would probably come here first.

I shot a quick text to Aunt Becky,

> Me: Safe at Fat Tony's. Hope you feel better.

then maneuvered up the wide stone steps, avoiding the groups of people gossiping outside and the cloud of smoke hovering to the left. Inside, the voices grew, a rumble of conversation thunder rolling through the dining room. I stretched on my tiptoes and scanned the tables. On the far side of the restaurant Ainsley sat at a red-and-white-checkered table, her books spread out in front of her.

I pulled out a chair and sat down. She looked up and smiled, dropping her pencil into the spine of her textbook and stretching her arms above her head.

"You must've gotten here super early to get a table. It's crazy busy in here tonight."

"Yeah, we all came here after cheerleading practice. I figured I'd just stay and wait for you guys to show instead of going home in between. I've had my history notes to keep me company."

"Well, I guess that explains the bow."

She looked puzzled, then snapped her fingers and yanked the gold and purple bow from her ponytail and shoved it in her backpack on the floor. Always the peppiest Lions fan, Ainsley could've just been wearing it to match her Go Lions T-shirt, but I guess not today.

"Thanks. I always forget about it way up there. I've lost three already this year by forgetting to take them off."

"No worries." I leaned across the table and tried to lower my voice, but the wall-to-wall sound made it difficult. "Hey, did the whole squad show up at the party on Friday?"

"Think so. Except maybe Amelia, because she's always working." She scrunched up her nose. "Why?"

"I just remember that you said you were hoping they would come. I saw Kate and a few others, but I wasn't sure about the rest of them."

"Yeah, which is really great. I don't know for sure if it made the difference, but they might actually let me have a part in the halftime routine next weekend."

Her smile beamed with neon-colored happiness. I knew this was a big deal, but I didn't get it. Top of the pyramid, bottom of the pyramid, it was all the same to me. But if it made her happy, then good for her.

"That's awesome. We'll all have to make sure we come to see you."

I rummaged through my bag and pulled out my notebook, then flipped to the page of names toward the back. I scrolled through the list and added a few more girls from the squad that I'd missed.

"How well do you know all the girls on the team?"

"You can't be serious right now. You think one of my friends could be on your list of suspects?" She wagged her finger toward the notebook dismissively. "If you don't know who they are, I doubt they had anything to do with it. You're being paranoid."

I sighed and slid the notebook back into my bag. "Right now it could be anyone. It could even be someone close to me. Someone I know really well." My eyes met Ainsley's. "Or at least someone I thought I did."

Cora's words rang through my memory. Maybe she knew something, maybe she didn't. I'd have to try and get her alone to see what she really knew.

"What are you trying to say exactly? You think I may have done it?"

"Well did you?" I cringed as the words came out, but I couldn't take them back. It had gone so well with Sasha this afternoon. I should probably just not talk at all anymore.

"Omigod, Brea. You seriously think I would do something like that? What would be the point?"

"I don't know, Ainsley." I leaned back and crossed my

arms. "I only had one drink all night and it was the one *you* gave me."

She screeched her chair back and crossed her arms. Other tables turned and stared. "I gave a lot of people drinks that night, and you're the only one who ended up in the hospital. How do you know it even had anything to do with that?"

"Because they found poison in my system. Something called nightshade. And since I didn't go around eating a bunch of plants, it had to be in that drink."

Ainsley stood up and leaned across the table, her perky ponytail falling to the side as her eyes burned holes through my head. "I don't know where my smart, level-headed friend went, but I am going to the bathroom, and when I come back, if this deranged episode of *Law & Order* isn't over, I'm leaving. You can explain your crazy to Sasha and Cora, because I know you're getting on their nerves too. Besides," she leaned in closer, a deep snarl across her lips, "if I wanted you dead, you wouldn't be sitting here."

She pushed off the table and the red pepper flakes rattled in their shaker. She strutted toward the back of the restaurant. I put my elbows on the table, my head in my hands. What was I doing? She was right. I needed to stop interrogating my friends or I wouldn't have any left.

Or maybe I just needed to stop asking at all.

I peeked toward the bathroom door and switched chairs. Ainsley's backpack sat open on the floor and I flipped through. Textbooks, makeup, a pill bottle. I read the label. Just her allergy medication. Then, in the middle compartment, a pink notebook with a Faraway

Lions sticker on the front. I pulled back the little elastic strap holding down the cover. Her journal. Perfect. I closed the other pockets of the backpack and slid back over to my chair, hiding the journal in my own bag. Maybe it would be nothing, or maybe it would help me figure some things out. Besides, underneath her sunny personality Ainsley seemed like she might have a dark, malicious streak after all.

"There you are."

I jumped and jolted the whole table as my knee hit the leg. Sasha and Cora took the two empty seats on either side of me.

Sasha tapped my shoulder. "Relax, girl. Ainsley here yet?"

"Yep," Ainsley said as she returned from the bathroom. She cleared her textbooks from the table and slid them into her bag while glaring over at me. "But, I'm not sure if I'll be staying."

I flashed her my sincerest puppy eyes. "You should. I'm sure we can find something else to talk about."

She crossed her arms, popped her hip to the side, and jutted her chin in the air. "Good."

The other two girls passed looks between one another, confusion ripe on their faces. Ainsley settled back down in her chair, her perfect smile flipping back on like the lights on a marquee.

"I'm starving. Did you want to order?"

"Wow, is that Malcolm over there with Jessie Taylor?" Sasha said.

I glanced over to the booth by the window. Malcolm Rogers sat with a striking senior girl. Laughing his most likable laugh. Smiling his most hypnotizing smile.

Oozing the same level of charm he'd cast on me less than a week ago—except from this angle it made my stomach queasy.

"Maybe they're, like, study partners or something," Cora said, trying her hardest not to stare.

Malcolm reached across the table and took her hand. Nope, definitely not study partners. However, this time seeing him with someone else had a bit less sting.

Sasha covered her mouth with her hand and tried to be covert, not like Malcolm would care if anyone gossiped about him anyway. "Well, it looks like you are the lucky one here, Brea. Considering how you saw him making out with someone else less than a week ago, this should be the final pin to pop that crush bubble."

"No worries. I think I'm over it. Plus, I've crossed him off my list."

Ainsley shot me a nasty glare. I hung my head and fidgeted with the cutlery as I pulled my legs back under my chair, half expecting her to kick me in the shin.

"Hey, Cora, didn't you kinda have a thing for Malcolm too?" Sasha added. "I thought you told me that once."

Cora cowered in her seat. "Not really. I think I'm over it too." She flashed me a smile, then flicked her dark hair over her shoulder, shielding her face.

Why didn't she just want to admit it? Clearly neither of us really stood a chance anyway—at least not a long-term one.

The door flew open again. Huddling in the doorway stood Declan with the same three friends from his locker this morning. They glanced around for a table and, for the briefest moment, Declan locked eyes with me across the crowded room. His expression soured and he looked away. His dark eyes flitted around like a squirrel suddenly caught in a trap, then he shook his head and charged back out the door, his friends calling after him as he left.

I backed up my chair and tossed my bag over my shoulder. "Hey, guys, I'm not really up to this right now. I think I should probably head home."

Sasha grabbed my hand, and her forehead crinkled as she forced me to make eye contact. "Is everything all right? This isn't about Malcolm, is it? Don't worry about him. There will be someone better for you. I'm sure of it."

I patted my free hand over hers then slipped out of her grip. "Not at all. Malcolm isn't even a blip on my radar anymore. I'm just getting a headache, that's all."

"Okay, then text me when you get home so I know you're all right."

"For sure." I rushed away and weaved through the tables, nearly taking out a server with a tray full of pop. He scowled at me, as did Declan's friends when I pushed my way through them to the door. I cringed at my total lack of manners. I'd been raised better. I knew it. But unfortunately, I needed answers, and they were already walking down the street.

13

———

I tore down the street, Declan's pace much faster than mine. I considered calling after him but I still hadn't figured out what I was going to say. Besides, if he really was up to something, maybe I could find out what it was first.

He wandered down the quiet house-lined streets, nightfall coaxing most everyone else indoors. The drying leaves on the trees rustled and fluttered in the hazy glow of moonlight that threaded through the streaks of gray clouds in the sky. I kept to the sidewalk, avoiding the piles of leaves collected at the edge of the neighborhood lawns and curbs. Crunching along as I walked would for sure get me noticed. He stopped in front of the park at the end of the block and slowly turned around. I ducked behind the Fisher's picket fence and held my breath as if he could hear it over a block away. The playground swings screeched in the dark as the evening breeze pushed them back and forth. I counted to ten. Once. Twice. Then Declan's footsteps started up again. I waited a few extra seconds before peeking back around the fence, but he had already disappeared.

Dammit.

I ran to the end of the block, a fifty-fifty chance of left or right. Except, there were no more footsteps and no moving shadows to provide a clue. I closed my eyes and let my gut guide me left, then headed down Hopkins Street hoping I'd made the right choice. I passed a half-dozen houses, but there was still no sign of Declan. I stopped and turned back, staring the other way, but didn't see any movement.

Footsteps pounded up ahead. I snapped back in that direction and followed the sound until I reached St. Michael's Church with its stained-glass windows and massive iron cross looming overhead. The gate on the back of the churchyard creaked and echoed eerily through darkness. I crept up to the side of the building, pressing my back against the stone and brick. It pulled and scratched at my back as I inched closer to the corner so I could see into the churchyard. The heavy shadow of the building blocked out the streetlights and cloaked the entire yard in blackness. I took a deep breath then peeked around the corner, my hands tight in fists and ready at my chest.

But as I turned the corner, there was nothing there.

I relaxed and shifted back toward the street.

"Are you following me?" Declan skulked out from behind me and I screamed. The sound reverberated off the building, causing even more fright. I clasped my hand over my heart as the beats pounded hard and fast.

"What makes you think that?"

"Because you've been behind me for about ten blocks now, and I want to know why." No humor edged his expression. His jaw clenched hard as stone.

"So maybe I am. But first you need to tell me why you've been avoiding me."

"Avoiding you? Since when do you care what I do? It's not like we're friends or anything."

The words came out fierce, but I noticed him flinch as he said them. Maybe he didn't like me being around, or maybe it hadn't all been just a dream.

"Since I got out of the hospital you've stayed away from your locker. You've skipped school. And if you are around, you're never alone. You always have your rebel-wannabe entourage with you."

"I don't know what you're talking about. Your chirpy friends are always with you, but I don't accuse you of anything. Maybe you're the one with the problem?" He paused, his mouth open like he had more to say, but then he closed it and tossed his hands in the air. "Forget this."

He turned around and stormed toward the street.

I started to chase after him, practically vibrating with all the nasty things I wanted to say in return, but instead, something different flew out of my mouth. "Is this all because of that kiss? Because you kissed me in that horrible midnight place and you didn't know if I'd remember? Well I do."

He stopped dead, his black boots slamming to a halt. "I don't know what you're talking about."

"If you didn't know what I was talking about, you would've kept walking."

"So what if I do know?" He turned around and the

anger faded into a new emotion that I couldn't read. Something I'd never seen across his always-stable face. "But maybe I've been avoiding you because I know it was a mistake."

That hurt. The pain of a thousand thorns ripping their way through my flesh, except this time I couldn't escape it.

"So instead you're just going to run? If you regret kissing me, that's fine, but I'm not letting you leave until you tell me what really happened. Where is the Midnight Realm? How did I get there? How did you get there? You said you weren't the one who tried to hurt me, but you don't give me any answers to help me believe you." I dropped my voice. The neighbors were likely ready to come yell us off the block. "And when we kissed, what was that pink spark? What did you do to me?"

Declan stormed back and stopped right at my feet, towering the several inches of height he had over me. "How is this my fault? Maybe you're the one who's hiding? I don't have that kind of magic. Why don't you tell me how you got there and how I got there, because right now I'm thinking you're the one who can't be trusted."

I rubbed my hand over my forehead and rolled my neck back, the stars far above me. "I don't know what you're talking about. I am just me. The stupid girl who let someone slip something in her drink and made a fool out of herself then woke up in a strange land, full of terrifying things, and the only person who knows anything about it is you." My eyes started to well up, but I pushed down the tears. He couldn't see my weakness. I wouldn't let him see it. "For some reason I believe that you wouldn't intentionally try to hurt me, even if this was your fault. But please, just give me some answers so I can figure this out." I pulled the neck of my sweater down revealing my shoulder, the black thorns ominous under the streetlights. "Tell me what's happening to me. Please."

Declan's jaw dropped open as he stared at the mystical tattoo winding around my arm. "I . . . I have to get out of here." He turned and ran toward the sidewalk.

I ripped my cell phone out of my pocket and hit the power button until it lit up. "If you don't tell me, I'll call the cops. I'll tell them that it was you who poisoned me. There are witnesses that saw you at the party."

He slowed down, possibly reviewing his options. "You wouldn't."

"Why not? You always talk about being a badass. Now you can have the juvie record to go with it. Or maybe they'll just try you as an adult since it'll probably be considered attempted murder."

I flipped to the keypad.

"Nine . . . one . . ."

"Fine," he shouted. "Just put the phone down."

I dropped it to my side but kept my hand wrapped around it tightly.

"What do you want to know first?"

I spun through the kaleidoscope of questions in my head. "How did you know about the Midnight Realm? And the Sluagh? And magic? What secret are you hiding?"

He hung his head to his chest and strode toward me

slowly, as if approaching his own execution. "Because I'm a nightmare."

"Yeah, I already figured that out." I pulled the phone back up. "I'm not kidding about the cops."

Declan grabbed my hand and pulled it back down. "No, like the real thing. Creatures that wander through people's dreams and feed off their energy. Nightmares."

I shivered and yanked my hand out of his.

"Brea, I'm a demon."

14

———

"A what?" I retreated closer to the church, as if that would even save me. I had no idea how to deal with these sorts of things. "Like a demon. Like a thing from Hell that takes people's souls?"

"Not exactly. Just calm down and I'll explain."

"Calm down? How am I supposed to calm down after you tell me this?" I paced, looking for the best route for escape. Through the churchyard would keep me trapped by the fence. Heading any other direction might be pointless as Declan's long legs would quickly catch me if he tried. My ribs compressed against my lungs, my breath coming shorter and harder, the blasts of mist in the cool fall air puffing like a steam engine.

"You are not allowed to be mad about this. Yes, I'm a nightmare, but you don't even know what you are. What kind of danger you put me in."

"What makes you think there's something wrong with me?"

"Your prissy pink magic and the fact that you have a

tattoo growing out of your arm. You are the last person who gets to judge me right now. For all you know, you could be the devil himself."

I stuck my hands on my hips and glared at him. "Do I seriously look like the devil?"

He glared back, his poker face much better than mine. "And do I seriously look like a demon?"

No, he didn't. He looked like any other boy at Faraway High. Except, maybe in the top twenty-five percent or so. I smacked myself in the forehead. *He's a demon, Brea. Stop thinking about how hot he is.*

"So, if you're a nightmare that means you were in my head, just hanging out in my coma?"

"Yeah, I guess. But it wasn't exactly what I'd planned either. I didn't know you were in a coma."

The night wind picked up and I crossed my arms, trying to hold in the heat. Or maybe the chill radiated from my bones instead.

He stuffed his hands in his pockets and jerked his head toward the street. "Let me walk you home and I'll try to explain."

He slowly walked toward the sidewalk and I rushed to keep up with him.

"Okay, first question. How did you become a nightmare?"

"It's not really something you become. It's more of who you are. My whole family are nightmares and we have been for centuries. It's not really much different than being human, except now and again we need to consume the energy of others. Kind of like a multivitamin, or something."

"Is that why you looked so sick at my party?"

He nodded and pulled his arms tight to his sides. I thought I saw him shudder, but it might have just been the wind. "I hate it. The feeling of invading someone else's space and taking from them. Then seeing them again and knowing the things they dream about, their wishes and fears and perversions. I feel gross, but if I don't do it, I'll die."

"Does it hurt? The people you steal from?"

"I don't think so. I've heard people talk at school after I've fed from them and they don't seem any different. A little more tired than usual. But sometimes if I stay too long, their dreams can turn on them. Dark things they bury deep inside their minds get loose when they don't have the energy to keep them locked up. It's a huge misunderstanding. We don't create bad dreams, we just bring them to the surface."

I let the facts settle and collect into the folders of my brain, filed away for later. The soft percussion of his heavy footfalls against the pavement, trailed by my higher pitched ones, blended into the whistle of the wind between the houses and the hum of the highway that passed on the far side of town.

Declan never looked at me, simply kept his eyes laser focused one step ahead of his feet. He maintained a respectable distance, never daring to swerve or potentially brush against me on the narrow sidewalk. I wondered though—chivalry or fear?

"So, if you don't create the bad dreams, does that mean I brought the Midnight Realm? That it was already inside my head?"

"I don't know for sure. But it makes sense. Do you remember ever having been there before?"

"I've never even left the state. My aunt keeps me close, and I think I'd remember going somewhere horrible like that."

"Yeah. I've only been there twice, but the feeling sticks with you."

"So where is it exactly?"

"Everywhere and nowhere, I guess. Realms are kind of like dimensions. They stack on top of each other like those Russian matryoshka dolls that all fit into each other."

"There are other realms?" I hadn't even considered it. The Midnight Realm seemed so foreign, like it didn't really exist. But of course, if it did, then the possibility that other realms existed wouldn't be unreasonable.

"Yes, but no one has been able to travel between them, at least not that I've heard of. Years ago they were all locked down, so when I ended up there with you I was plenty shocked." His eyes flitted back and forth as his brain processed, then he nodded as if convincing himself of something. "Maybe you are right, it was all in your head. Just a really vivid dream."

We turned the final corner toward my house. A bluish glow danced on the front lawn from the light of the television through the window. I slowed down, still so many things left to ask, but I wasn't sure of all the questions. At least not yet. We reached the front walk in silence and stood staring at anything but each other.

"Can you please not tell anyone about my secret? If people knew, they would all run screaming, and my family would probably have to move."

"Sure. I won't tell anyone." I glanced up, his dark eyes drifting, lost in a sea of his own thoughts. Telling me his secret broke him down. Slipped the postured reputation from his stance and left a scared boy with nowhere left to hide.

"Thank you." His lips curled into a partial smile, the other half still adrift. "I'll try to help you figure out what happened and what's going on with your arm too."

"That would be great. Thanks."

I looked down at the cracks in the sidewalk and rocked back and forth on my toes, trying to think of anything else I could ask. For some reason, the walk home seemed too short and I half considered asking if he wanted to take another lap around the block, but he probably had other places to be.

"I should likely—" I turned my gaze up from the ground and caught him staring. Close. Close enough to feel his warm breath falling on my cheeks. Too close.

Glimpses of his lips on mine flipped through my brain. His hands running up my spine. His arms holding me tight. I needed to shake these visions, but right now they haunted me, drawn out by his unrelenting dark stare.

The front light of the house burst on and I jumped. Either the 9:38 timer or someone creeping on us from inside, both telling me to move along and let him leave.

"I better go." I pointed at the door then shook my head and started up the walkway. When I reached the front steps, Declan cleared his throat behind me.

"Brea," he called, still standing in the middle of the sidewalk. "I lied before. I don't really regret kissing you. When I see you, it's the only thing I can think about."

My head hung down toward my chest, the chill leaving my cheeks. "Yeah, me too."

He smiled, the lines of his teeth glowing bright in the moonlight. "Good night, Brea."

"Good night, Declan," I whispered. But he was already gone.

I dragged my feet down the hallway, my toes barely lifting from the tiles as I shuffled toward my locker. Last night I had tried to sleep. After pouring through entries in Ainsley's journal, my eyes began to droop and my fingers felt double their size as I turned the pages. Maybe the hopelessness of finding nothing in Ainsley's ramblings gave me a sense of safety, or maybe my body just gave up. I lay down on my bed, turning off all but the lamp on my nightstand, and closed my eyes. Seconds later, though, they pinged open wide, my brain tossing out memories like parade candy to entice me into that dark world. Alone and scared.

I searched the Internet for calming techniques to help bring on some rest, but that turned into searching Ainsley's social media along with the accounts of half a dozen other kids from school, then researching everything there was to know about nightmares. Granted, that last idea hadn't helped matters at all as the search images that popped up had only added more cards to my deck of insomnia games.

I emptied my textbooks into my locker and swapped them for my English notes. The clunk of the books against the metal bottom seemed exceptionally loud for first thing in the morning. Next I pulled out the pink journal and held it in my hands. A sharp pain stabbed through my diaphragm. All that for nothing. Now I needed to find a way to get it back. I stashed the journal on top of the other books. Maybe during cheerleading practice I could slip into her locker and she'd never know.

Bang.

The locker door clanged against the adjacent one as Declan appeared beside me.

"Hey."

"Hey, yourself." I grabbed my head and blinked, the excitement bringing on a dizzy spell, but I forced it down.

"Are you okay? You look pretty rough."

"Thanks." I leaned against my neighbor's locker, letting the bank hold me up. Less work for my legs.

"I've been thinking about last night . . . a lot." His lips curled into a half-smile, and he glanced up and down the hall as if someone might see and it would ruin his perfectly awful reputation.

"Yeah." I thought a lot about it too. Besides the tortuous research, everything he'd told me had been the truth about his condition. Coupled with the fact that he pretty much saved my life, he'd fallen off the list of suspects. Or maybe I kind of liked how I felt when he was around. My cheeks warmed, the lack of sleep clearly getting to me. "So, what about it?"

"I told the rest of my crew to let me know if they find out any information on who poisoned you when they are—" he winked "—out for dinner."

"Thanks. You didn't really need to do that, but I appreciate it."

"No problem. But, it probably makes sense for you to give me your number, just in case they find something. That way I can text you and let you know." He handed me his phone.

"Really? That's a pretty smart idea." I texted myself, then added my name to his contact list. "But only in case you have some information." A giddy smirk split across my face as I handed back his phone, and willing it to stop just twisted it into an even more cringeworthy look. *Real smooth.*

He scratched the back of his head and looked down. "Yeah, of course. Or, you know, if anything else comes up."

"Yeah, of course."

My hands suddenly seemed awkward and not sure what to do with themselves. He rocked slightly forward in his boots, the soft woodsy smell of him taking over my senses and not helping with the dizziness.

"Are you okay there, B?"

Declan pivoted away from me and the air thinned again. Sasha stood behind him, her hip popped sharp to the left and a dangerous don't-even-try-it look on her face. Cora stood behind her, tucked out of the way to watch the show.

"I'm fine, Sasha. Declan just needed . . ."

"Mr. Richter's e-mail address. Need to beg for an extension on that Hamlet essay."

She tapped her foot, looking from me to him and back again. "You know they're all on the student portal of the school website, right?"

Declan shrugged. "Forgot my password. Too lazy to make a new one."

He slid out from between us and moved back toward his own locker.

Sasha took his spot beside me and leaned in. "Seriously, what were you doing talking to him?"

"Just asking him some questions and trying to figure out if he had anything to do with my coma. That's all."

"Oh, it sure looked a lot cozier than that. I told you he's a bit of a predator. Maybe you should try to get a new locker assignment or something?"

"He's harmless. And he had nothing to do with whoever poisoned me. I'm sure of it."

"Really? He kinda gives off that I-bury-bodies-in-my-backyard vibe."

"I said it's fine, Sasha. Just let it go," I snapped.

She recoiled, her eyes wide in shock. "Wow, someone's a bit edgy today."

Cora's mouth dropped open and she slammed her hand over it to stifle her giggle.

"Well you know what, Sasha—"

"I can't believe you." Ainsley marched down the hallway, the click of her shoes echoing off the tile like gunshots.

The knot in my stomach tightened and I hunched forward.

"What's wrong, Ainsley?" Cora asked as she came to an abrupt stop in front of us.

"Why don't you ask Brea, the klepto?"

"What are you talking about?" I asked, my stomach almost completely cramping up.

"Seriously? I spent all last night trying to find my journal, and then this morning Mackinley told me she saw you rifling through my stuff while I was in the bathroom at Fat Tony's last night. I know I had it when I got there, and then when I got home it was gone. Don't lie." She crossed her arms over her chest, her lip sticking out and demanding answers.

"I don't know what you're talking about. I looked in your bag for a pen, that's all, but I didn't take anything. Maybe it fell out on the floor or under your car seat or something?"

"Open your bag."

I breathed a sigh and opened the flap of my book bag. She dug around inside and scowled when the book didn't appear.

"See? I told you, I don't have it. Why don't you tell me what it looks like and we can all keep an eye out for it."

Her attitude deflated, still angry, but not sure how to direct it anymore. "It's a fuchsia moleskin with a Lions sticker on the front."

"Like that one?" Cora pointed to my open locker behind me, the journal sitting right on top of all my books. Shoot. I had wanted to move it, but then Declan came and I forgot.

As Ainsley reached past, her fist nearly swiped the side of my face. She grabbed the journal from the locker, ensuring to knock me in the head with it as it came out.

"Yup, this is it. What do you have to say for yourself?"

I looked over at Sasha and Cora. Their eyes hardened to stone, likely to try and match Ainsley's.

Ainsley shook her head as her beautiful face turned ugly with disgust. "I don't even care. I thought we were supposed to be friends, but you've been super weird since you got out of the hospital. I hope something didn't get all rattled up in there." She flicked her hand toward my head, then turned on her heel and strutted her way back down the hall, the sound trail of her steps following behind.

I slammed my locker shut and tried to follow, but Sasha grabbed my arm and held me back.

"Brea, why would you steal from Ainsley?"

I considered lying. It might be easier, but Sasha would see through me in a second.

"Fine. So I stole her journal. I admit it." I tossed my arms wide open. "I was trying to see if she was the one who poisoned me. She's not, by the way."

"You need to stop this. It's getting out of control."

I ripped my arm from her grip. "Must be easy for you to say. Have you ever spent three days in the hospital? Where your family didn't know if you would live or die?"

"No, I haven't. But I don't need to almost die to know that this obsession is going to destroy you."

"Or are you trying to cover something up?" My head swam, colors and sounds beginning to blur together. "You're the one who keeps insisting that I drop it, but maybe you're the one I need to look out for. You're the one who threw the party in the first place. It happened at your house. Is there something you need to tell me, Sasha?"

Sasha exploded. "Are you kidding me?" She tossed her book bag down to the floor and got up in my face. Her olive skin smeared, her head stretching and contracting in front of me.

I blinked, squishing my eyes closed hard to clear my view. Sasha's face morphed back to normal, just even more angry than before.

"I did you a favor by throwing you a party, and now you think I tried to kill you? I've only been trying to help you. But I don't even know if I'm qualified for the help that you need."

An odd sting rushed through my body and the whole world fell even more out of focus. "I don't need your help."

A pink light flickered. My hands lit on fire. Arms wrapped around me from the back. Woodsy smell. Declan.

"Hey, that's enough now," he whispered in my ear.

His arms eased and my knees buckled. He tightened his grip again. "I think you've had enough today."

My head fell back against his shoulder. He was probably right, except the day had only just begun.

16

———

*T*he school secretary, Ms. Collins, pushed open the door to the first aid room. "Are you feeling any better?"

I sat up from lying on the lumpy plastic-covered mattress. "Yeah, I think so."

She placed her hand on my forehead then looked me over. "Looks like you could still use some rest. Maybe I should call your aunt and send you home."

I slipped my cell phone out of my pocket and jiggled it in the air. "Why don't I just call her myself. It'll save you the time."

Her stare narrowed, the wing-tip eyeliner curling up even higher on the sides.

"This isn't just a way to get out of a test or something, is it?"

"Ms. Collins, I've been on the honor roll every year and I am probably still in the top five percent of my class. I can't afford to skip a test if I want to get into an Ivy League school, now, can I?"

She grinned. Either the answer had satisfied her or maybe just the prospect of doing less paperwork made her happy enough to let me slip. I dialed all but the last number to my house and pulled the phone to my ear.

"Hey, Aunt Becky. I'm not feeling well, so I think I'm going to go home and sleep. Is that fine? Uh-huh . . . Uh-huh . . . Okay. Bye."

I powered off the phone and slipped it back into my pocket before she could see the keypad screen. "Looks like I'm good to go."

I jumped off the bed. A wave of dizziness flooded over me, but I kept upright and marched right past Ms. Collins and out of the office.

Outside, the sun beamed down on the glistening tops of the pumpkin-spice-colored trees. It seemed too happy of a day for how lousy I felt. The fight with Sasha played on a loop in my head—at least the parts I remembered. The nasty things I said to her. Getting caught with Ainsley's journal. Almost lighting up some unknown magic in the hallway. Each little thing ticked a box on my checklist of problems, and it only seemed to be getting longer. If Declan hadn't jumped in and stopped me, who knows what I would or could have done? I'd have to thank him if I ever had the guts to go back to school again.

I stood on the sidewalk in front of the school. Aunt Becky worked late tonight, so she'd still be at home. How would I explain this to her? Sorry, I had to leave school because I almost barbecued by best friend? Not likely. I needed to get myself together and start fitting these puzzle pieces into place. Going home might be the smartest idea, but my feet didn't feel like being smart.

Instead I wandered through the quiet streets of Faraway, trying and failing to focus my thoughts. Brain fog rolled in thick and heavy. Maybe I could just close my eyes for a little bit? Set an alarm for every fifteen minutes until I rested enough in total to function? Nothing bad could happen in that amount of time. Could it? Even though Declan told me the Midnight Realm was probably in my head, it actually made things worse as it would be even easier to access than I originally thought.

"Whoa, watch where you're going." The mailman swerved off the sidewalk as I nearly ran him over, lost in my own thoughts.

"Sorry," I shook my head and stopped. Where was I even going? Up ahead, a charming little sign hung beside the sidewalk. Two tiny bluebirds sat atop the fancy capital T of "The Danley's," which was painted in a delicate flowing script. Maybe I had somehow ended up right where I needed to be.

The quaint home stuck out from the others on the street, resembling a rustic Tudor cottage instead of the cookie cutter craftsman style houses that lined the sidewalk. I pulled back the knee-high garden gate and took the winding walk to the front door. Most of the garden had been trimmed down for fall already, but a few orange chrysanthemums and purple asters still hung onto the soil. Toadstools and tiny figurines peppered the garden. Angels, pixies, princesses with tiny crowns. I'd have to come by in the summer to see it in full bloom.

I knocked on the front door, the sudden urge to run away building strong. I didn't know if she would even be able to help, but the way Mrs. Danley had looked at me with her knowing grin at the hospital felt like a connection.

The door opened to Margaret's husband, James.

"Hello there. Can I help you?"

"Is Mrs. Danley home? She helped me out at the hospital a while back, and I was hoping I could talk to her for a few minutes, if that's okay?"

His wrinkled face softened at the recognition. "Ah, you're the Coma Girl."

I cringed. Even the elderly had adopted that nickname. "Yeah, that's me."

"Well, come on in. Margaret and I were just sitting down to tea. Would you like a cup?"

A cup of tea would probably be wonderful, but I didn't have time for the soothing effects. I doubted they wanted to drag a sleeping girl off their floor. Besides, I had a new policy about taking drinks from strangers. "No, thank you. I won't stay long."

He led me down a narrow hallway to a sunroom at the back of the house. Light streamed in through all the windows, and the whole room glowed like a teahouse in Heaven. Chamomile mixed with the tartness of wild berries hung in the air, and I swallowed as my mouth watered. Knickknacks and other treasures filled the room like a museum, each one unique yet somehow fitting in with the rest of the aesthetic. A cross-stitched plaque hung over the door frame.

Look within to find your truth.

"Look, darling. We have a guest," James announced.

Margaret turned away from the windows, her smile

beaming as I approached the small table. "Breanne, dear. Please have a seat."

I pulled out the cushioned metal chair and sat down, the damask tablecloth draping over my legs.

James tapped me on the shoulder. "I'll be back with the tea. Are you sure you wouldn't like a cup?"

I shook my head and he disappeared back into the hallway.

Margaret smiled, her shaky hands folded neatly on the table top. "It's lovely to see you up and about. Have they discovered what happened to you yet?"

I ran my fingers over the handle of the delicate floral teacup in front of me, the cool porcelain smooth under my fingers. "No, and that's kind of why I needed to talk to you. Did you see anything or anyone suspicious when I was in the hospital?"

"Oh, honey," she reached over and put her wrinkled hand on my arm. "You are far too young to let the badness of the world consume you. Let the police do their job and try to move forward. It's for the best."

My stomach ached, and I shifted in my seat. She sounded like Sasha. "Maybe you're right, but there's something else that's been bothering me. Ever since I woke up, things have been very different for me. Strange."

"Strange how, dear? You're going to need to give me a bit more if you want me to help."

I laced my fingers in my lap and stared down. How was I going to be able to explain this when I didn't even fully understand yet?

"Like you aren't feeling well, or you're seeing things, or something more abstract, like magic?"

"Magic?"

She grinned and eased back in her chair. "Ah, so that's it."

"I mean, I don't know. Maybe. I'm not really sure yet. But . . . you believe in magic?"

"'Course I do. Just because most people don't believe doesn't mean it's not real. There are a lot of weird and mystical things that happen here in Faraway. People just choose not to see them."

"Yeah, I've been starting to notice that myself."

She pointed her finger in the air and shook it like a detective finding a clue. "I always knew you were a special girl. Been keeping an eye on you all these years. I always know the special ones." She held up a small plate. "Cookie?"

"Sure." I scanned the delicious spread of treats on the plate and settled for the one with a chocolate castle printed on the side. "You've been watching me?"

"Oh, don't get your knickers in a knot, my dear. All of your awards and recognitions are in the newspaper. Plus, you only live a few blocks away. It's not like I'm tapping your phones or reading your diary. I just like to know what's going on in town."

"So, you knew that I had magic and you didn't tell me? Do you know why, or what I am?"

"That, I'm afraid, is not something I've quite figured out. However, I'd appreciate it if once you do know, you could tell me. I don't always know the source, but I can tell when things are out of the ordinary. Even the way you arrived here as a child set off my alarm bells."

"Arrived? I don't remember anything special about it."

Bits and pieces of scenes filled my head, like a movie spliced and sped up. The hallway with the torn purple carpet at Aunt Becky's apartment building where she used to live. The rough hand of the care worker who dropped me off. My pink unicorn backpack and long pigtails.

"You probably don't. But it was a strange night indeed. A blackout covered the entire town. Three full hours of not a spark of electricity anywhere around. Then, miraculously, all the lights came back on."

"Big deal. Blackouts aren't super common, but I wouldn't call that unusual."

"Really? Except there wasn't a breeze. No storm or even a drop of rain to cause it. The utility company never figured out why it happened. No downed power lines, no power surges, no explanation for any of it."

"Maybe it was just a coincidence?" I broke the cookie in half and put a piece in my mouth, the chocolate melting almost instantly.

"Maybe. Or perhaps it had nothing to do with you at all. Perhaps it had something to do with the other little girl, exactly your age, who was adopted in Faraway the exact same night. The same night all the lights went out without reason."

"Another girl?" I scooted to the edge of my chair, running through the faces of people I knew. I never talked about that night, so it wasn't surprising that maybe they didn't either. "Does she still live here? What's her name?"

"Yes. A feisty little child. But I haven't heard much about her lately. Like you said, maybe it was just coincidence."

"Do you know her name?"

She tapped her finger on her chin and stared at the ceiling for a moment. "Yes, I believe her name is Cora Murphy."

Cora? It couldn't be. Her words played out in a loop in my head. *Maybe it was someone a lot closer than you think.* Was that a confession instead of just a warning?

"Thank you, Margaret—I mean, Mrs. Danley—but I think I need to go."

"Well then, I hope I helped answer some of your questions."

"I think so."

She pushed the plate closer to me. "Take another cookie with you. I shouldn't be eating them all anyway. Plus, promise me you will go home and get some sleep. You look absolutely knackered."

I nodded, but sleep was the last thing on my mind. "Thank you. You don't know how much this means to me."

"You're welcome."

I raced toward the front door, nearly plowing over James and the elegant floral teapot that matched the cups in the solarium.

"Slow down, young lady. The world will not move faster because you do."

I helped straighten him up. "I'm so sorry. But I really need to go. I'll let myself out."

He shook his head and chuckled. "Youth."

As soon as I hit the front step, I pulled my phone out of my pocket and texted Declan.

Me: Think I know who poisoned me. Can you meet? Need to talk.

I waited for a few minutes, but he didn't answer. School still had a few hours left to go, so maybe he was still in class. Either way, my sudden burst of energy came with a price. One of my best friends wanted me dead.

17

Before opening the front door, I checked my phone for the hundredth time. Still no messages. Why couldn't he choose today to cut class? I knew he'd skipped so many times before. Why not when I wanted him to?

Inside, Aunt Becky puttered around the kitchen humming to herself while making a ham sandwich. She'd already attached her Rebecca Vardan name badge to her blouse and probably only had a few more minutes before she needed to leave. Perfect.

"Hey, Aunt Becky."

She jumped and dropped a butter knife on the floor, the metal clanging against the tile. She clasped her hand against her chest. "Brea, don't sneak up on me like that. You scared me."

I picked up the knife and handed it to her. "Looks like visitors."

She squinted then continued to spread mustard

across the bread. "Since when are you superstitious? You've always been almost a little too practical."

I shrugged. "I don't know. I guess I just haven't been feeling like myself lately."

"Is that why you're home so early? If skipping class is part of the new you, I'm not very interested in seeing more."

I pulled one of the kitchen chairs away from the table and flopped down on it. "No. I didn't feel very well. I've got a headache and I figured I could maybe come home and get some rest."

She placed the back of her hand against my forehead. "You don't feel warm. But that doesn't always mean anything. If you're going to sleep, I can leave Tori a note to be quiet when she comes home."

"Thanks." I stretched my arms above my head, the yawn coming naturally and not needing to be faked. "Don't worry about me. I'll be fine."

"Actually, I kind of need to talk to you. I have a surprise coming for you tomorrow."

"A surprise? For me?"

"Yeah, it's . . . well, it's kind of hard to explain. I . . ." She crouched down in front of me and took my hand, a stone expression falling over her face. She stared up at me, her eyes analyzing and picking me apart. "Never mind. You look exhausted, and this conversation needs to happen when you're in a better place. We can talk about it in the morning after I get back from work."

I wrapped my fingers around her cold hands and squeezed. "Are you okay, Aunt Becky?"

"Yeah." She stood up and pinched the small spot at the top of her nose between her eyes. She looked away.

"I'm fine. I just want you to know that I love you so much, and anything I've ever done is to protect you and keep you safe and happy."

"Of course I know that."

"Good." She nodded and resumed her sandwich making, cutting it diagonally and packing it in a plastic container. "Now, go get some sleep and don't worry about anything. It's a good surprise. I promise."

I arose from my chair and rubbed Aunt Becky's shoulder as I headed out of the kitchen. What kind of surprise would get her all worked up like that? Something to protect me? Dread flooded my bloodstream. Was she sending me away? She said it wasn't safe for me here after what happened, but maybe it didn't matter. I ran up the stairs and sped into my room, closing the door behind me. All the more reason to expose the poisoner before Aunt Becky or anyone else made any snap decisions.

Letting my head fall back against the door, I slid down to the carpet, my knees folding up to my chest. Would she really get rid of me that easily? She wouldn't be the first to abandon me. Maybe I was the real problem. Declan said my memories of the Midnight Realm existed in my brain already. Maybe this wasn't the first time my weird uncontrollable magic had gotten me into trouble?

I slid the sleeve of my sweater up. The line of thorns had grown and twisted up my forearm, branching into additional vines. I needed answers, and fast. My butt vibrated as the text message signal muffled between my jeans and the carpet.

I slid my phone out. Finally.

> Declan: Sure. I have news too. Too dangerous to text. Meet me in the soccer field behind the school. 9 o'clock?

My fingers flitted across the screen.

> Me: Perfect.

The three little bubbles popped up immediately.

> Declan: See you then. :)

I laughed and slid my phone back in my pocket. Declan definitely didn't seem like an emoji kind of guy, but apparently everything I knew about him was wrong anyway. I pushed up from the floor and stuffed pillows under my comforter in case Tori felt like checking up on me. Then I sat at my desk, tapping my foot, and waited for Aunt Becky to leave.

18

I pulled my jacket tighter around me as the wind in the empty school parking lot whipped up. Lights still illuminated the football field, but I didn't see any purple and gold bodies running on the glowing patch of green. Practice must have either just ended or someone forgot to shut off the floodlights, meaning the school would be in for a huge electricity bill on Monday.

I crossed the lot and huddled close to the side of the school away from the wind. I checked my phone: 8:45. Still a bit early, but maybe Declan would show soon and we could move somewhere warmer. The soccer field seemed like the most random place to meet, but at least it would be private.

After pulling the hood of my jacket over my head, I raced around the corner, slamming right into a brick wall with a yellow lion mascot on his chest. Griffin Carlisle, school running back and hometown hero.

"Whoa. Where are you going so fast?" he said as he straightened me back up.

I kept my head down. "Sorry. Just going to meet someone."

"Practice finished about a half hour ago, and I'm the last one out of the locker room. Unless you're here for the caretaker, everyone else is gone."

I glanced up into his sparkling blue eyes. No wonder half the school had a crush on him with those classically handsome good looks. But tonight was about dark things in shadowy corners, not pretty boys in football cleats. "No worries. They're probably not here yet."

"Are you okay?" A girl's voice came from behind him. She stepped out and linked her arm with Griffin's, his purple football helmet dangling from her free hand.

"Yeah, just fine." I stepped to the right, and she moved with me, looking me over. Did I really look like that big of a hot mess? "I really gotta go."

She shrugged and looked at Griffin, then let me pass. "If you're sure everything's okay."

"Absolutely." I swerved around her and kept walking past the gym doors toward the fields.

"Why do you always think you need to help everyone, Ari?" Griffin's voice echoed behind me.

"Force of habit, I guess. Besides, you totally love me for it."

Even with the distance between us I could hear their lips smacking together. I cringed as if I were watching instead of just walking away from the intimate moment that I did not need to be part of.

Once I cleared the school building, the wind picked up again, but I had no time left to stay sheltered. I rushed out past the lines of metal bleachers into the grassy fields beyond. Past the soccer fields sat empty lots and a rarely used set of train tracks leading farther into the Midwest. I pulled my phone out: 8:51. At least the stadium lights calmed my nerves.

And suddenly, *clunk.* The entire schoolyard went black. I should've known. I set my phone to flashlight and swept the area all around. Nothing but yards of grass and white painted lines. I flipped to the text screen.

> Me: Already here. Are you coming?

> Declan: Be right there. Five minutes.

I slid my phone back in my pocket and listened to the silent song of the night as my head kept piecing the puzzle together. Things I knew for sure were the things I was most afraid of. Declan was a nightmare. I'd been to or heard of the Midnight Realm before but had no idea why. Cora arrived in Faraway the same night I did and might be tied to everything. And the one thing I'd been hiding from the most—I had some sort of magic that I couldn't control.

I looked around again—no one coming—then held my hands tight together. So far, every time I'd seen that pink spark was when I focused hard on something. The kiss with Declan. The argument with Sasha. Maybe if I focused my energy and emotions, I could do it on my own.

Closing my eyes, I took a deep breath, visualizing the oxygen flowing into my lungs and throughout my body.

It worked in the yoga class I took at the YMCA with Tori. Maybe it could work now. My breathing slowed and my heart pumped in an even, languid rhythm. *Here goes.*

I stared at my open hands and focused on the lines of my knuckles and the fortune lines across my palms. A warm tingle started in my shoulders and bled across my chest and down my arms. The tattoo of thorns prickled against my skin. I flinched but tried to hold steady. A faint glow started in my hands, pink and sparkly, like gum blowing into a bubble except brighter and hard to stare at directly.

The bubble grew and grew until it hovered above my hands, floating in the air.

Excitement blended with the magic, and the colors seemed to change, melding and swirling as the ball of light expanded.

My legs started to shake. Energy drained quickly from my limbs, considering I didn't have much to give in the first place. A slow clap thundered in my periphery and I shot my head to the side. The bubble popped. Light fractured into shards and dissolved into the night sky.

"Impressive. She finally figured it out," rang a female voice.

Two figures rushed toward me, one tall and the other much shorter with long hair slapping behind them like a cloak.

I pulled out my phone again to the flashlight. Declan, his expression grave as he walked militantly across the field. To his left, Cora, her lips in a wide smile and her right hand clasped to Declan's arm as she cuddled up beside him. My open hand turned to a fist, rage exploding in my cells and ready to attack. He knew. This whole time he'd played me. They'd probably worked together to poison me. Evil partners in crime.

I rushed toward them, shining the flashlight into their guilty faces.

"How could you?"

Declan opened his mouth, but Cora wrenched on his arm and he winced. Something in Cora's left hand glinted in the flashlight beam. A long metal blade poking right against Declan's abdomen.

19

"So, it was you this whole time?"

Cora coaxed Declan closer, his feet stumbling forward, but I couldn't keep my eyes off the knife in her hand. About ten inches of metal shining vile and dangerous in her dainty fist. Did she even know what she was doing with that thing?

"Oh, Brea. You say that like you had no idea. I practically came out and told you the day you got back from the hospital. But I guess you didn't pay attention to me then either. No one ever pays attention to me."

"Well, you have my attention now. What is this all about?"

She tossed her head back and laughed, the sound light but tinged with something more sinister. A victorious cackle of sorts. "Is that all it took? Putting you in the hospital didn't work, but the second I mess with your boyfriend you're all ears. So typical. So shallow."

She jabbed the blade harder against his stomach. I

jumped forward as Declan groaned and caught his breath, stiffening up taller.

"I'm impressed, though. A nightmare, Brea? I never pictured a good girl like you falling for someone more my style. But maybe bad boys are trendy again or something? I realized when you were cozying up with him this morning that you'd probably already started figuring things out and it would only be a matter of time before you came for me." Her hair blew dramatically in the wind. "If you haven't noticed, I prefer to strike first."

I held my hands out in front of me, my heart pumping loud as my brain tried to connect the dots while surveying our escape options. Unless Cora dropped the knife, they seemed pretty limited without at least some bloodshed. I glanced at Declan, his eyes glued on his captor as he stood rigid in her grasp.

"Why are you doing this? I haven't done anything to you. And if I have, tell me so I can make it right."

"Make it right? How are you going to make years of being Brea and Sasha's 'other friend' all right? Always the extra one. The leftover. Forget the fact that I've been plotting this since I was a kid. Everything you've ever done has driven me to want this more than anything. Everybody loves you. You're so smart, Brea. You're so pretty, Brea. It's exhausting. Plus, you don't even deserve it. I'm only 0.3 GPA points behind you, but nobody cares. You didn't even notice me enough to accuse me of poisoning you. You ripped into your own best friend before you even considered asking me if I'd done it. Thanks a lot."

"I didn't accuse you of poisoning me because I didn't think you could be this cruel."

"Yeah, right." She rolled her eyes and shook her head, then waved the blade toward me, her hand still tight on Declan's shoulder. "You mean you don't think I'm capable of something that cruel. No one does. Everyone underestimates me, but I'm actually quite talented. I weaseled my way into your little friend group. I coaxed Malcolm to come to the party as a distraction so I could poison your drink. He's an amazing kisser, by the way." She turned to Declan. "You've got a lot to live up to there, Dreamlover."

"That was you on the deck at the party?"

"Of course it was me. And again I was reduced to 'random girl making out with Malcolm.' I might as well be a ghost around you. I'm only there to be used when you need me and then cast aside like a gum wrapper. But that's going to change."

Declan moved in my periphery. A slight nod of his head commanding my attention. I slid my gaze to him, slowly, trying not to set Cora off. His eyes burned wide and wild, embers stoking for a raging inferno. He needed time to make his move.

"So why did you wait? You said you've been plotting this for years. Why go through the trouble?"

"The magic, silly? It wasn't just yours that was bound until *your* sixteenth birthday. Every other fairy on Earth had theirs bound too. Waiting for you to have your happy birthday so they could be whole again. I couldn't just kill you without getting my big payoff first."

"Fairies? Seriously?" I laughed then covered my mouth with my hand, but I couldn't stop. "Like butterfly wings and pointed ears? I'm sure that would be a great look for you."

Cora growled and stomped her foot. "It's not funny. It's true."

A flash of movement. Declan twisted out of reach and ran left. Cora lunged and swung the knife, but the blade whistled through the air just behind his back.

Cora sighed and swiped her hand dismissively toward him. "Whatever. Run away. I don't care. I only needed you to get her here." She pointed the knife toward me, a delighted grin breaking across her maniacal face.

"Brea, run," Declan yelled. He flailed his arms toward the parking lot.

I watched her. If I chose a direction, she could give chase, but Declan would be right behind her. If she'd come this far, she'd be too calculated to be clumsy. There had to be an end game I wasn't seeing.

She flipped the knife up and twirled the sharp pointed end against her index finger. "Yes, Brea. Run. Go ahead."

"What's your game, Cora?"

"No game. I just have something you want, and you have something I want, so I bet we can make a reasonable trade."

"And what's that?"

She shrugged. "Knowledge. Unlike you, I grew up knowing exactly who I was and what I was. Youngest daughter of the darkest fairy the Realms have ever seen. I just need you to send me home and help me get everything I deserve."

"Home? Like the Midnight Realm? The one you trapped me in for three days?"

"I knew it. I knew you were lying when you told me

you didn't remember anything. You're such a liar." She stormed forward, the knife pointed right at me.

"Don't do this, Cora." I backed up, my hands out, ready to strike if I needed to. I'd taken on a Sluagh before. I could do this.

"I wasn't trying to trap you anywhere. I tried to kill you. You were supposed to die and open all the locks."

She swiped the knife at me. I jumped back, the blade slicing a line straight through my jacket.

"Stop it. We can figure this out. You don't have to kill me."

"Yes, I do. This is bigger than either of us. I need to finish it."

Cora charged again, the knife sliding across my left arm. A line of fire raged across my forearm. Blood pooled and splattered on the ground.

"Stop moving," Cora screamed.

I clutched my arm over the wound. My fingers slipped against the wetness.

The wind picked up, whipping between us. Booms of thunder clapped. The sky flared.

Cora grunted and jabbed again. I swerved out of the way, my left leg tangling around my right. The knife missed. My stomach slammed into my throat. I fell.

I hit the ground, the impact jolting pain through my spine.

The horizon lit again. Green and red. Bolts of lightning speared the clouds. The sky split open. Rain poured.

I scrambled back onto my hands as Cora loomed closer, my fingers slipping in the wet grass.

"Please don't do this," I screamed.

Cora leapt at me and I rolled to my side, but she never landed. Declan wrapped an arm around her torso and yanked her back to her feet. She jabbed behind her with the knife, rain dripping off their faces, but he turned and smashed her arm against his knee. The knife dropped to the ground.

Beside me, the air crackled. I pushed up on my elbows as a silver swirl sparked and spun between us.

"What is that?" I yelled as I struggled to my feet.

Declan and Cora stopped fighting, his arm locked tight around her neck. Both of them stared at the silver vortex growing in the air.

Thunder rumbled above. Water streamed down my face as my clothes and hair became plastered to my body. The vortex grew.

As I stepped closer, the center widened and déjà vu slammed me like a car crash. Slashes of red sky appeared over a dark, dead forest. Shrieks and howls gushed out and scattered on the wind.

"It's a portal," Declan screamed over the noise. "We need to close it."

The Midnight Realm. I couldn't breathe. The world shrank. Tight. Claustrophobic. I gasped as a haze fell over my vision. It couldn't be.

"It's the blood." Cora's tinny laugh rang through the field. "The keys to the kingdom were always in your family's blood. I should've guessed."

I dropped to my knees and ripped at the blood-stained grass, then tossed it into the wind, scattering the pieces.

"What are you doing?" Cora howled. She lurched forward, but Declan held her back.

The vortex contracted. I ripped more. Rain flowed down my cheeks and off my chin as I rubbed the water through the grass, washing the dirty blood away.

Slowly, the portal grew smaller. Each inch that disappeared eased the tension in my limbs as I desecrated the ground to force it shut.

Blue light glowed beside me. Cora's hand illuminated in a familiar spark.

"Declan, look out."

She flicked her arm back and the light knocked Declan to the ground.

"No!" I screamed, but he shook his head and struggled to his feet.

Cora snatched the knife from the ground and charged at me. I leaned back. My pulse thrashed in my ears. She swung. I screamed. The pink spark blasted from my hands and tossed Cora back onto the ground.

Declan grabbed the knife from her hands as the vortex disappeared with one last flash of silver light.

Rain dripped off me as I swayed on my knees. Cora scrambled to her feet and limped off toward the parking lot. I tried to shout after her, but the words jumbled in my brain and stuck somewhere between my tonsils and my tongue.

Declan reached for me, but I couldn't feel my arms to reach back.

"Brea, are you okay?"

I heard the words, but they floated somewhere far away.

Declan kept calling my name, but I couldn't answer. My tongue stayed glued to the roof of my mouth. The world faded out of focus. Distant. Hazy.

My shoulder hit the ground. My head. The smell of wet grass. The smell of my own blood.

20

———

"Declan, I'm going to be okay."

He finally let go of my waist as I pushed in the front door, nearly falling into the house.

"Don't tell me you will be fine. I watched you drop back there and I'm not leaving until I know you're okay."

I opened my mouth to argue but slammed it back shut. Arguing with him would get me nowhere, and we needed to come up with a plan to deal with Cora anyway.

"Fine. Tori must be out, since her car isn't in the driveway, but she could be home any minute."

I peeled off my jacket and hung it by the door. The damp chill from my storm-drenched clothes seeped under my skin, freezing me down to my bone marrow. I jerked my head forward and raced through the house, not stopping until we reached the safety of my room.

"So what are we supposed to do now?" I darted over to my desk and flung open the drawer, searching for a notebook and pen. Things always made more sense on paper. "First, we need to figure out where Cora disappeared to. Then, I think we need to know exactly what Cora means by 'fairy.' Maybe Mrs. Danley knows something about them. Or maybe we can talk to someone you know. Or maybe—"

Declan covered my writing hand with his, stopping the pen in its fevered track.

"First, I think you need to take a breath." He pulled the pen out of my grip and tugged it closer to him, his arms resting around my shoulders. "You're a complete mess right now. Even if we did find her, you might need magic to stop her, and I don't think you can handle it in this state. We know what we're up against now. You need to get some sleep and recharge or you'll be useless."

I twisted out of his arms and paced the far side of the room. "But what if she comes after us tonight? We need to be ready."

"Even if she does, you can barely stand up."

"Of course I can." As the words flew out, the room began to spin. I slapped my hand onto my head as my knees buckled and I jerked forward. "I'll be fine."

"Brea, what's going on?" His stern frown softened to concern, his dark eyes warm like smoldering coals in a midsummer campfire. Comforting. Familiar. And a little bit dangerous.

"Cora is trying to kill me. That's what's going on. We need to figure out why she's doing this. What she wants." I took a breath and blinked the dizziness down. "What her next move is."

"I know that. I mean, what's going on with you? You've fainted twice today. You don't sit still. I know you're being threatened, but this isn't you. You've been completely manic."

"I said I'm fine," I barked, but I lurched forward, still spinning. Tears flowed but I didn't have the strength left to stop them. I turned to face the wall. To hide. "I can't sleep. I haven't slept since I left the hospital."

"Are you kidding? That's been like four days. How are you even functioning?"

"Maybe I've dozed off for a few minutes here and there, but every time I close my eyes, I'm scared that I'll end up in that place again. The Midnight Realm among the monsters."

"Monsters like me."

"No, no, no." I shook my head, but it made everything worse. A haze fell over the room and I grabbed onto my dresser to keep upright. "You aren't one of them. You're one of the good ones."

Declan grabbed the back of his neck, staring at the floor. Whether he believed me or not didn't change anything. He wasn't the evil thing he thought he was. I'd seen the good in him. If only he could see it himself.

He pulled off his hoodie and draped it over my desk chair. His black T-shirt clung to his skin, the sleeves cutting tight against his biceps as he pulled the staged pillows out from under my comforter and flung them on the floor. He smoothed the covers out then lay down, his head propped against the headboard.

"Come here."

"What are you doing? Tori could be home soon."

"It doesn't matter. You have a problem, and it's something I can actually help with." He raised his arm and curled his fingers in a beckoning wave. "Please, come here."

I crept over toward the bed, each step unsure, until I sank into the mattress beside him.

"Take off the wet sweater. You can't warm up if you're still soaked."

Declan faced the far wall as I unzipped the sweater and dropped it on the carpet. A sharp chill pulsed through my limbs. I shivered, but then started to warm up again as I lay down next to him.

He wrapped his arm over my shoulder and curled my body against his, my head landing square in his chest.

"I'll stay awake and watch over you. If you tremble, or move, or even breathe wrong, I'll jump right in your dream with you and pull you out."

"What if it doesn't work?"

"Then I promise we will go find Cora and take her down. But, please, let me help you. You can't do everything all by yourself."

I wanted to argue. I wanted to tell him again that I would be just fine, but as the warmth of his skin bled through his thin T-shirt and the soft thump of his heart beat against my ear, the arguments started to float away.

He rested his chin on my head and squeezed his arm tighter around me. My eyelids began to close, the light fading into the distance as the scent of wet cotton and sandalwood blanketed over me, tucking me in. Declan hummed a song I'd never heard, yet it still sounded strangely familiar. The buzz vibrated through his chest and lulled me deeper into slumber.

I relaxed my hand, the cut from Cora's knife still

tingling in my forearm, then spread it across his stomach as each of my muscles released one by one, no longer able to fight anymore. His fingertips traced the tattooed briar of thorns now wrapping completely from shoulder to wrist, and I melted into his touch.

"Sweet dreams, Brea," he whispered. Or maybe I just dreamed it.

21

———

*R*ays of morning sun painted warm stripes across my face. I arched my back and stretched my arms out. A tiny squeal escaped my lips as a pleasant tingle rippled through my nerves.

"Does that mean you had a good sleep?"

I startled at the sound of Declan's voice rumbling above my head. I leaned back as his tired eyes stared down into mine.

"Sorry, I totally forgot you were here."

He swept the stray hairs off my forehead and smiled, a contented perfect smile that coaxed my lips to curve up in response.

"Then I'd say my plan worked. No bad dreams?"

"Not that I can remember."

He nodded, gazing down at me.

"Thank you. I needed that so much. Even my brain seems to be functioning better now. It isn't running at ten thousand RPM anymore."

"Good, because we're going to need your smarts to figure out what to do next."

I slid up and sat facing him. I liked how he looked in the early light of day. Even exhausted, the morning haze stripped off a layer of attitude, leaving behind a hushed kind of handsomeness. Like a bite of peanut butter and jelly or your favorite sweater just out of the dryer. Simple, yet completely magic.

I skimmed my hand against his cheek. He leaned into my palm and closed his eyes, murmuring something I didn't understand. His hair drooped messy over his face as the sun teased streaks of dark copper from his cappuccino waves.

"Thanks for saving me from myself."

I leaned closer and brushed my lips lightly against his. Just a taste. An invitation.

He curled his arm behind my back and pulled me in, his lips pressing back harder, responding better than any words could try.

My cheeks burned as I tangled my fingers in his silky hair. Our first kiss had been a desperate one—all shallow breaths and heat and sweat—but this kiss didn't need any of the buildup. It dragged along, lazy and slow, a whole conversation unfolding without speech or reason, just letting us enjoy the moment for however long it might last.

Declan drew back. "Are you sure you're okay? I don't want you to think that I'd ever try to take advantage of your condition. I might be evil, but I'm not a total monster."

"No. I never thought that. And you're not evil, no

matter what you think. Maybe just a little bit in the gray."

He took my hand and laced his fingers through mine, staring longingly, yet a bit sad. "So what's our next move? Do we go straight for Cora, or do we try to figure out what she meant by 'fairy' and if it actually has anything to do with your magic?"

"I'm not sure. What do you know about fairies?"

"Not a lot. Fairies run like royalty through the realms. They have their own society and rules, but perversions like me and my family aren't welcome. They are why the realms were locked in the first place."

"Then maybe we should start there." I rested my head on his shoulder and rubbed my thumb across his knuckles. "And stop worrying about who you are. You might be considered a demon, but to me you've always been an angel."

A knock rapped on my bedroom door. I scrambled to sit up straight and Declan jumped from the bed, grabbing his hoodie and retreating to the farthest corner of the room.

"Brea, are you up?"

I rushed to my feet and straightened out the covers, smoothing my hair back and adjusting my clothes. "Yeah, just a minute."

Tori didn't listen and the door flew open as she marched across my floor. An older, well-dressed couple followed behind her.

"Who are they?" I asked.

No one that I knew wore a tailored suit that nice outside of a wedding or funeral. Perfect blue pinstripes and an impeccable matching silk tie seemed completely out of place for this town. The woman stood tall and rigid, her hands clasped politely in front of her form-fitting dress, which matched the shade of blue in her partner's suit.

"Um . . . first, maybe you need to tell me why there's a boy cowering in your closet?" Tori wagged her finger into the corner, and Declan slipped out from behind my closet door to join us.

The strange woman gasped and clutched her partner's arm, her waves of blond hair shimmying as she shuddered.

"You have a nightmare in this house," the man said, glaring at Declan.

Tori shook her head and blinked. "Forget that. You need to explain how a boy got into your room first thing in the morning."

"Through the front door, Tori. Where's Aunt Becky?" I spat back.

"Maybe I should just go." Declan started toward the door, but I walked over and grabbed his hand. The strange man frowned and shook his head.

"Brea, you are more responsible than this."

"Tori, this is so not what you think."

"Maybe you should leave," the elegant woman said to Declan.

"Your aunt hasn't come home from work yet. She was supposed to be here when they arrived."

"Who are you to tell me what to do?" Declan argued back.

The woman clutched her hand to her throat. "I'd watch your tone, young man."

The voices swirled, everyone bickering all at once. I

tossed my hands in the air and yelled, "Tori, who are they?"

The room dropped into silence, everyone staring any place but at each other.

Tori cleared her throat and placed her hand on my shoulder. "Brea, these are your parents."

22

"What? My parents disappeared over twelve years ago. This must be a mistake."

I glared at the couple standing prim and proper by my door. It couldn't be, could it? Yes, the woman's shade of blond looked similar to mine, as did her thin lips, and his eyes shone the same shade of crystal blue that stared back at me in the mirror every morning. But those were simple things. I could look like a lot of people. Did I even want it to be true?

"No mistake, Brea. These are really them." Tori nodded her head and forced a reassuring smile, but it provided little comfort.

"You knew about them? And you didn't tell me?"

Tori dropped her hand, shock and shame glazed over her face.

The strange man claiming to be my father raised his open palm. "We swore her to secrecy. It's not her fault."

"Then it's your fault. You abandoned me for my

entire life, and now you think you can order people around, keep secrets from me, then just show up here and expect me to listen to you? You can't be my parents, because clearly you know nothing about me."

"Breanne," my maybe-mother said, her voice low and calming, "if you will let us explain, you will understand why we had to do what we did. It's not as simple as it sounds."

"Then explain. I'm sure there had to be a good reason to give up your own child. I can't wait to hear it."

"I don't think it's appropriate to discuss this in front of him." She nodded toward Declan.

I squeezed his hand tighter. "He means more to me than either of you right now, so maybe leave him alone."

"But, he's part demon. He can't be trusted."

"That's not your call."

Declan's hand fell away from mine. "I'll just go. I told you before, no matter what I do I'll always be the bad guy. Nothing is gonna change that."

"But . . ."

He didn't let me argue. Instead he placed a kiss on my forehead and marched out of the room, glaring at my parents on the way out before slamming the door behind him.

"Real nice. This isn't the best way to gain my respect."

My father frowned and let out a deep sigh. "There are so many things you don't understand, but we will try to explain. I promise."

Tori shuffled in between us, blocking the questioning stares shooting back and forth. "Before you start, I'm going to head to the inn and see if I can find Becks. She should probably be here."

"Thank you, Victoria. That would be very helpful," my father said as Tori slid behind him and followed Declan out the door.

The three of us stood silent, analyzing each other, pondering our next move like zoo animals finally free in the wild.

I threw my hands on my hips. Clearly my courage didn't come from these two. "I guess I'll start then. Where have you been for the last twelve years?"

They looked at each other, wordlessly drawing straws, my mother losing the battle. She stepped forward. "We've been living in Rhode Island. We wanted to be closer, but we knew that being here would put us all at risk. We didn't want that for you."

As she spoke, her stare concentrated on my arm. The light green of her irises flitted back and forth following the vines up my flesh. She tiptoed closer and reached toward my arm. "May I?"

I swung my arm forward and she grabbed on, tracing the thorns with her finger. Her forehead wrinkled, and she turned back toward my father. "Daniel, it's all the way down her arm. We should have come sooner."

"Do you know what it means?" I asked.

"Yes." She steered me toward the bed and I sat down as she twisted my arm back and forth to examine it more closely. "You've been using magic, haven't you?"

"Kind of. It all just sort of happened at first, but it seems to be getting stronger."

"And it will, until you either take control of it or it consumes you. You are more powerful than you know, but the power is controlling you, not the other way around. These marks are a warning that the magic owns you."

I snapped my arm out of her grip. "Owns me? Then how come I managed to take out a dark fairy if I wasn't in control? Fight the Sluagh? I can handle so much more than you know."

"Sluagh? That shouldn't be. They were banished years ago," Daniel said.

"You definitely are a little late for those kinds of details. This girl, Cora Murphy, she cut me. Opened a portal and tried to kill me last night." I stuck out my other arm, showing them the snake-like cut across my skin, dried blood still caked in the wound. "This is the second time she's tried it. Poisoned me at my own birthday party and put me in a coma, which sent me to the Midnight Realm."

My voice started to crack as the memories flooded over me. The harm my once-friend had done. The betrayal stinging my eyes and hurting my soul.

"Maybe if you'd come sooner, you would have known that."

"Who is Cora?"

"Someone I thought was my friend. She said she was some kind of fairy, and she was using me to take what's hers. Except I don't know what that means."

They glanced at each other, a dark cloud brewing between them.

"This is what we need to tell you." My mother retreated to my father's side. "I'm Bridget and this is Daniel, King and Queen of the Realms. You are our only daughter and the Crown Princess."

I laughed. "Are you kidding me? I've seen some

pretty crazy things the last few days, but this is ridiculous."

"It's true." Daniel knelt beside the bed and took my hand. I flinched in his grip but relented. "Your mother and I ruled the fairy court and all the realms outside of Earth, including the Midnight Realm. One of our subjects, a dark fairy, built an army to overthrow our reign. They wanted to unleash the beasts in the Midnight Realm to Earth and conquer the humans instead of maintaining the balance we had fought to keep for thousands of years. A great war ensued, and she put out a bounty on you, our only child, to ensure that it would end our line and she could claim the crown for her and her family. Instead of risking your life, we locked down all the realms only to be reopened by our family."

"That's what Cora meant about needing my blood, wasn't it? She can't open the portal without it?"

He nodded. "But, hiding here on Earth didn't stop the threats. Any monster that had escaped before the lockdown or that already dwelled on Earth came for you. Our magic called them like a beacon and put a target on your back. We made the decision to keep you safe, so we sent you to live with my sister and used every last drop of our own magic to bind your powers and the powers of every other being on Earth until the time you could take your place as the rightful Queen of the Realms. We gave up everything to keep you safe."

I pulled my hand away and headed to the far side of the room, pacing small circles as I held the sides of my head. All this information threatened to explode brain matter all over my carpet. "I can't be a queen. I'm still in high school. This has to be one giant mistake."

"Of course you can," my mother said. "Just because we weren't here doesn't mean we haven't been watching you. Rebecca has told us all about your wonderful life. You've grown up smart, beautiful, and strong. It's all we ever wanted for you. You will make a great queen, and we will be by your side to help, but in order to get everything back to normal, you need to claim the crown and own your destiny."

"Own my destiny? You sound like a terrible graduation speech or a cheap fortune cookie. I am owning my destiny, and it doesn't have a crown in it. I'm going to Princeton. I'm going to practice law or be a doctor or sell insurance—it doesn't matter. I can't be a queen. And why did you wait until now to tell me? Cora seems to know exactly who she is, but I don't."

My father rose from the floor and thrust his hands in his perfectly tailored pockets, the gravity of the situation seeming to be completely lost on him. "We wanted to wait as long as possible. Just because your magic was coming back didn't mean you couldn't have a few years of a normal life before you needed to take the throne. Besides, telling you would've made you easier to find. There are things out there that can access your thoughts, your hopes . . . and your dreams. They would betray you in about five minutes."

"Declan wouldn't betray me. He's a good person, no matter what you think. If you'd let him speak instead of throwing him out, you'd know that."

"Maybe you're right, but there is too much on the line to make a mistake. If what you're saying is true,

Cora is our biggest threat right now. If she truly is the daughter of our greatest enemy, she'll try to claim the crown for herself. She can only do that by ending our line. In other words—you." He pointed at me, then dropped his hand to his side.

"So how do we stop her?"

"We can't do much without any magic. You need to claim the crown first, then you will have the power of the Realms and she will be no match for you. However, if she destroys you first, our family claim will die and she will be able to take your role as queen. If she's anything like her mother, that would mean unleashing Hell. No one here on Earth would survive."

"Then give me the crown. If it'll stop Cora, I'll take it and figure the rest out later."

"It's not that simple. You can't assert yourself as queen on Earth. You will need to go to the Midnight Realm to get it."

"No. I can't go back there. There has to be another way."

The door burst open and Tori ran in, her mascara running down her face. "Becks is gone. I found her purse and keys lying on the ground beside her car and this attached the window."

In her shaking hand she held a yellow Post-it note. I charged toward her and hugged her, then pulled the note from her hands.

Aunt Becky's with me.
Meet me at MIDNIGHT.
-Cora

———

23

"What does that even mean?" Tori sobbed harder. I handed the note to Daniel then squeezed Tori as her tears soaked my shoulder.

"It means the dark fairy struck first. She's going to use Rebecca to open a portal to the Midnight Realm." Daniel groaned and rubbed his temples. "Poor Rebecca. Always in the middle."

"You put her in the middle," I snapped at both of them, my own tears falling and turning my room into a watery haze.

"I know." He hung his head, remorse for all his bad decisions finally bleeding through. Except, this epiphany of his came way too late. Too late for me. Too late to save his own sister.

"So, that's it then? Cora's going to open a portal with Aunt Becky's royal adjacent blood and make a run for the crown, then try to take me out?" A simple plan. If she succeeded, I lost my life, and if she failed, I still lost the one person I loved more than anything in the world. How did everything get so screwed up? Last week I was panicking about making sure I got an A on my calculus test. This week my life was a sick prize to be fought over, no matter who or what made up the collateral damage.

"Let Cora take the crown. It won't do anything as long as you're still alive." Bridget swept my hair back over my ear. I flinched. Who did she think she was? They couldn't just walk in here and be my family. I had a family—Tori and Aunt Becky. They were the ones who held me when I was sick. They took me to my first day of school. They put up with all my crap but loved me anyway and pretended like it didn't matter. They were my real family. These people were so far behind in that race, they would never catch up. Being royalty didn't make you right.

"We can't do that. Cora has Aunt Becky. Once the portal is open, she has no use for her anymore." My stomach twisted and all my muscles clenched tight, aching to unleash fury on Cora but not knowing where to start. Aunt Becky would be helpless in her wrath. She had no idea what the Midnight Realm could do to her. The creatures that lived there. If it weren't for Declan, I never would've made it out alive, and that might have all been a dream. This was real. Real blood. Real terror. Real death. She'd never make it against the Sluagh, and they probably weren't the worst creatures hiding in that place. My tears came faster. Phantom pains stung my arms and legs where the thorns had cut me. The knuckles broken against the skull of a Sluagh itched. My left shoulder muscles severed by their deadly claws twinged. "I don't care about your stupid crown. She'll die in there."

Tori wailed and I buried my head in her hair, breathing in the smell of her skin. I couldn't let Aunt Becky die. Not because of me.

I gasped against my haggard breaths and cleared my throat of the salty tears I'd swallowed. "I'm going after her."

"No, Brea, you can't." Tori tugged me closer, but I pulled away and wiped the back of my fists over my eyes.

"I have to. I survived it once. I can do it again."

"But your magic," my mother said. "You're not fully in control of it. This isn't a good idea."

"If I don't try, Aunt Becky dies. If I do, then maybe she has a chance."

Daniel straightened up. "I forbid it. It's too much of a risk. If you don't make it, the realms will be in chaos. Your mother and I don't have any magic left to reclaim them. There is an order to these things that must be followed."

"I don't care." I marched up to him and glared into my own eyes. Aunt Becky's eyes. "I've followed the rules all my life. I've worked hard. I've done the safe thing. And look what happened. My entire world just landed upside down in less than a week because everyone followed the rules. And now Aunt Becky might die because of it. I don't care about the rules anymore. If the whole world crumbles. Great. Fine. As long as Aunt Becky is safe. As long as the people I love are safe, then let it fall."

I snagged my phone off the nightstand and headed for the door. "Tori, can you to drive me to Sasha's?"

"Of course." She wiped her tears and followed behind, her hand on the small of my back.

My parents stood, mouths open, in the middle of my room.

"Where are you going?" my father called after us.

"I'm going to get my aunt back and save the world you abandoned. Just like you abandoned me. If you want to come, you're welcome to follow."

I trudged down the stairs, the pieces of my plan falling into place in my brain. My parents hurried behind, my mother's heels clacking down the wooden steps.

"You know that's not what we wanted to do," my father said, trying to catch up.

"We can discuss apologies later. Right now I need to make a phone call. Someone I care about once told me I need to let people help."

***

Tori's Camry pulled into Sasha's driveway and I flung open the door before it even came to a full stop. My parents pulled in behind, driving Daniel's impeccable black Lexus. The gravel road off the highway probably cut at his soul in a car like that, but it kind of felt like payback for years of not being there for me.

"Just stay here. I'll be right back."

I knocked on the door and waited. I hadn't been back to Sasha's since the night of the party, which felt like years ago instead of just a week.

She opened the door, and her face scrunched up in disgust as she crossed her arms in front of her. "What are you doing here?"

"First off, I'm here to apologize. I should've listened to you when you said you had nothing to do with poisoning me. I know you're not the one who did it, but even if I didn't know, I shouldn't have snapped at you like that."

Sasha sighed and her shoulders fell forward as she backed up to let me in the house. She leaned against the open door, her arms locked across her chest and her lips pursed tight. "I told you I'd never hurt you, and I meant it. You're my friend. Or at least you were until you went all paranoid."

"I know, and it's my fault. A lot of stuff has been going on, and I thought I could handle it by myself but I couldn't. I should've trusted you."

She nudged her chin forward, her toe tracing through the thick front carpet. "You should've."

"And I promise I will do whatever I can to make it up to you. I love you, Sasha."

She burst out laughing then hugged me tight. "You're so dramatic, B. But I love you too."

I squeezed her as hard as I could until she gasped in my grip. "I missed you."

"Don't you ever pull that stuff on me again."

"I promise. But now I'm wondering if you can do me a little favor. I'll be sure to pay you back for this one too."

She let me go, her hands dropping to her hips. "What now?"

Of course, this wasn't the best timing for her to give

me anything, but apology or not, I needed her. Hopefully, if she was on my side, I just had to beg less.

"I found out that Cora was the one who poisoned me at the party."

Sasha's jaw dropped and she slapped me on the shoulder. "Shut up. Seriously? How could she do that?"

"It's kind of a long story. One that I will explain in detail when I can, but right now she's kidnapped my Aunt Becky and I need to get her back."

"Geez, B. Why didn't you call me about all this stuff? Mad or not, I still care about you."

"I know. I'm getting better at asking for help, and that's why I'm here. I need a spot away from town to deal with this. Any chance you'll let me trespass in the woods behind your house for a bit?"

"Sure. But what's with the whole entourage?" She pointed at the cars behind me.

"Um, that's Tori and my birth parents."

"What?" She lurched forward, the shock barely fading from the last surprise.

"Yeah. Like I said, long story. But can you do one more thing for me? Watch through your back window, and if you see anything come out of those woods other than us, lock yourself in the basement and call the police. Okay?"

"This isn't anything illegal, is it? Your parents aren't mob bosses or drug dealers or something?"

"No, but just promise me you'll do it?"

She nodded.

Perfect. One thing falling into place. There were so many things I needed to repay Sasha for, and I would spend the rest of my days making sure I did. When I got

Aunt Becky back, I'd make sure things would be different.

"Did you want to come meet my parents?"

"Sure." She smiled and closed the door behind her, then followed me down the driveway. Music bumped down the street. The heavy metal guitar and scratchy voices loomed closer as a silver Civic drifted on the gravel and screeched to a halt behind the Lexus. Declan stepped out of the passenger seat while his three nightmare friends followed behind him.

"You can't be serious?" Daniel said as Declan glared at him with his crew.

"Without any magic left, you can't help me. But Declan knows his way around the creatures of the Midnight Realm, and if I'm going to storm the castle, I need to bring an army."

"But—"

I raised my hand. "But nothing. He's coming."

Daniel huffed, but Bridget took his hand and stared him down. "Well, she's stubborn like someone I know. Go get her the Lacerine."

Daniel clicked a button on his remote and the Lexus chirped as the trunk popped open. He disappeared behind the car and resurfaced with a long silver sword in his hand.

"What the fresh hell?" Sasha said, her eyes bulging as she watched my father brandish the weapon in her driveway. "You owe me huge for this, B."

"I know. I know."

Daniel came around the car and held the hilt out to me. Rubies, emeralds, and sapphires wrapped around the handle and partway up the blade. A collector's piece.

Definitely more of a museum find than something tossed into the trunk of a midsize car.

"The Sword of the Lacerine. Take care of it. It's been in the family for generations, but it may help."

"Do you always carry a sword around with you?" Declan asked.

"When it has to do with my daughter, I do." He glared at Declan and Declan beamed back, reveling in the joy of getting under the man's skin.

"All right," I clapped my hands and headed toward Sasha's backyard. "Time to fight a monster."

24

Fire trailed the path of the sword across my flesh. The polished silver of the Lacerine's blade stained crimson by my own blood. I let the red pool on my palm, then squeezed my hand over the ground of the clearing.

I held my breath as the silver vortex appeared, smaller than a quarter but growing with intensity.

My mother stared at me with wide, sad eyes. "Are you sure you want to do this?"

"I have to."

A sharp sting pierced through my chest. We hadn't met in the best circumstances, but if I didn't survive, I'd never get the chance to know them. My parents. The ones that brought me life, even though their reign might be the reason I could lose it. I closed my eyes and made the promise to at least try to see their side if I made it through.

"Now, you all know your positions. Sasha and Tori are not to leave the house unless something happens and you need to get them to safety. As soon as Declan and I are through the portal, rip up the ground beneath it and wash away the blood with your water bottles until it closes. If anything comes out of the portal, run."

Declan's crew nodded, as did my father, standing at the ready on the path leading back to Sasha's house.

Declan glanced over at me, fear pouring out of his stare, or possibly just my own reflecting in his eyes. He took my hand, lacing our fingers together as the portal opened wide enough to enter. The red sky ahead of us flared a warning to turn back, but I couldn't. Not until I found Aunt Becky. I took a step in on shaky legs, straddling the world I knew and the one I dreaded. No going back.

The dead grass beneath my feet whistled as we walked through the open field not far from where we last left off. Shielding my eyes, I searched the sky, expecting the crows of death and the Sluagh to be close behind us. Nothing appeared except the moon. Unchanged. Unmoving. A static bystander to the horrors of this awful land.

My hand trembled on the hilt of the sword, knocking the blade against my leg. Every muscle, every joint of my body tensed, waiting for an unknown attack that I knew would eventually come. Did Aunt Becky feel the same when Cora dragged her into this Hell? Was she even still alive?

Declan tugged on my hand and pulled me out of my head. "Hey, it's going to be all right. We'll get in, then get out." He smiled, but the edges of his mouth wouldn't turn up. The same thoughts as mine likely ran through him, except he tried harder not to let them show.

I exhaled and looked down for a moment, collecting every ounce of strength before taking my next step.

"Get in, get out," I whispered as I plunged farther down the path toward the castle.

"So when we find your aunt, how will we get back?" Declan asked.

"My father said the crown will give me all the power I need, if I can get it. If not, my plan is to try to open another portal with my blood and bring us all back."

"But you haven't tried that here. How do you know it won't end up taking us to a different realm entirely?"

"I don't. But it's the best I've got."

Other realms. If I ever made it out of this one, I'd need to know more. How many were there? Were there worse things out there than what I'd already seen? What did it all mean?

Declan nudged my shoulder. "That's too bad. I was kind of hoping we might have to kiss our way out again."

I wanted to laugh, but I couldn't. It felt wrong. A kiss seemed foolish when facing death. But if it meant that I could have one more kiss with Declan, it might be worth it.

"Maybe. But I'd kind of like to save my lips for a victory kiss."

"Sounds like a plan to me."

Screams and wails moaned behind us as the briny sea blew salt in our faces, stinging my eyes. We kept a quick pace, not risking staying in one spot too long, but also not racing ahead too quickly. Playing safe in an unsafe world.

The bridge to the castle rose up over the sea—wide,

rickety wooden planks leading out over the tumultuous waves. I stared forward as I took a step. And then another. The boards creaked loudly beneath our feet, and my knees shook as we kept moving farther and farther away from the solid shore and over the unforgiving water. I looked out to the horizon. Heads and horns peaked over the waves, swimming in circles, closing in around the castle as we approached. Unknown creatures out there, watching us. Stalking us. Waiting to be fed.

Large spindly towers reached into the bloody sky as we neared the castle. Spikes lined the stone edges of the roofs and windows. No creature—human or otherwise—was welcome to climb their way in. But anyone dumb enough to try wouldn't even get that far. The building itself seemed to move. It slithered back and forth like a nest of snakes devouring the walls. My legs and arms shook as I recognized the sharp, triangular points sticking out from the castle walls. Not snakes. Thorns.

"What is that?" Declan said, pointing toward the moving briar.

"Remember when I told you about the man-eating vines?" I jutted my chin toward the castle. "That's them."

He glanced at me. "And you escaped these before?"

"Yeah. And I guess I'm going to have to do it again."

I held up the Lacerine and charged toward the end of the bridge.

The vines snapped out a few feet from their nest, whipping past my hands. I reeled back. They snapped again but couldn't reach.

I lunged forward and sliced through one of the thick vines with the sword. It cut clean. The pieces fell with a crash to the bridge, rattling the boards. I grabbed onto Declan's arm and steadied myself again as the two pieces replaced themselves with a new set of thorns.

I sliced again, one set dropping and another growing almost instantly in its place.

I cut again. The vines multiplied.

"How are we going to get through this? They're too fast."

Declan held out his hand and I gave him the sword. He stepped forward and ran the same test, cutting open a vine and watching it regenerate. He looked back across the bridge. The Midnight Realm stretched out behind us.

He lowered his head and whispered. "Do you trust me?"

I placed my hand on his cheek and stared into his dark eyes. "Yes."

He held the sword over his head, his elbow bent and ready to strike. "Then run."

Declan rushed forward with the sword, chopping and slicing as fast as he could. I stayed in close behind him, the thorns closing as quickly as they were cut down. My flesh burned as thorns ripped along my arms and legs, but I kept plunging forward, knowing that one missed step could mean getting dragged in.

We ran and ran, the few meters to the castle entrance stretching into miles. A vine snaked around my ankle and I screamed, kicking it with my other foot. Declan swooped back with the sword and sliced it clean as I kept moving forward, the rest still attached to my ankle.

Declan surged ahead, clearing the path as I stumbled after him, not daring to look back. The vine around my ankle slithered up my leg. I kept moving. Pain seared through me.

Up ahead, light finally appeared. I pushed harder, working against the throbbing. The vine slipped higher, circling my other leg.

Declan burst through the briar and into the castle, still hacking at the writhing vines around us. As I crossed the threshold, the vines on my legs clamped together. I fell forward, both legs wrapped and bleeding from the thorns.

"Declan," I screamed.

He spun toward me and grabbed my arm. "Brea, hang on."

The thorns wrapped tighter and jerked me backward, toward the briar. Declan's hand slipped and I whipped away from him, clawing at the ground. My fingers skated across the granite tiles.

Declan swung the Lacerine at the thorns. Sparks flashed as the metal clanged against the floor. The thorns dug into my thighs, and as the pain exploded through my legs, I screamed again.

Declan chopped at my feet and rolled me over, slashing the rest of the vine into tiny splintered pieces.

I crawled forward, but Declan hoisted me up, his arm clamped tight around my chest.

The briar slithered and slipped behind us with a hissing sound that rang through the cavernous room. Our panting breaths mixed with the sound—a frightening overture foreshadowing the danger that might still lie ahead.

"Are you all right?" Declan said, trying to hold me

steady on my feet. I grabbed onto his shoulder and limped forward.

"I think so. Let's just keep moving."

We stumbled on, Declan supporting my weight and inching me up the aisle toward the gigantic throne at the end of the hall. Stacks of skulls were gathered around the base of the charcoal throne, its intricately etched back stretching up as far as I could see. No roof covered this room, just a courtyard with the red cloudless sky boring down.

In front of the throne, a lump of blue quivered on the floor. Blond hair splayed out in a fan, bright against the dirty gray tile. Aunt Becky?

I limped toward her and collapsed on the ground. I shook her as my hands trembled.

"Aunt Becky. Aunt Becky, it's me, Brea."

She groaned and rolled over, her makeup smeared across her face and her eyes wet from tears.

"Brea? Is it really you?"

I pulled her into a hug. "Yes, it's me. I'm so glad you're all right."

"Brea, the things in here. I . . . I . . ." Her body shuddered in my arms and vibrated through me.

I smoothed her matted hair off her forehead. "I know. Now let's get you out. Declan, the sword."

Aunt Becky eyed the jewels. "They came for you. Your parents."

"Yes, they did, but let's talk about that later." I sliced my hand and dripped the blood on the tile.

Nothing happened.

I squeezed harder, more blood pooling on the floor. "C'mon, c'mon, c'mon."

Still nothing.

"I guess that makes sense," Declan said. "You've been bleeding all over this place and it hasn't opened anything. We need a new plan."

"Okay." I sat back and concentrated, hoping the magic I didn't understand would help get us out of here again. I closed my eyes and held out my hands, waiting to feel the rush of supernatural surge through me. If ever I needed magic to work, this was the moment—only I'd never had the chance to practice.

But wasn't I born to do this? To be queen?

A tingle started in my shoulders and squirmed through my bloodstream toward my wrists. Faint. Slow. Building ever so gradually. A small flash came from behind my eyelids. I glanced at my hands. The familiar pink spark appeared. The ball of light spun between my palms as it grew larger and larger, spinning faster and faster. The energy flowed just beneath my skin. Waves converging into one concentrated point. The light grew. My arms trembled from the force. But it kept growing and growing, then—*poof*—it blinked out, leaving us in darkness.

I smashed my fist on the floor. Tears welled in my eyes. I took a deep breath and centered myself to try again.

A dark shadow loomed over us. I glanced up into the sky as something moved above our heads. Something big.

The smell of rotting waste ripped through the throne room as the thing lowered down before us. Wind swirled from its wings, blowing me back against the skull throne.

A tail, thick and scaled like an anaconda, slammed down on the floor followed by four massive feet with minivan-sized talons.

I held my breath and clung to Aunt Becky as she curled into my lap. A mighty roar screamed around us and I covered my ears.

"She didn't," Declan yelled into the chaos.

But she did. I dared to look up. A tri-horned head glared down at me—Cora, perched between the wings of the dragon, a silver crown ringed on her head.

25

"Cora, what do you think you're doing?"

I scrambled to my feet, pulling Aunt Becky up. Her knees shook as she huddled against me and I held her close. Declan raised the Lacerine toward the dragon, but even a sword three times its size would be no match for this beast.

"I am taking what is mine. My family should have taken the throne over sixteen years ago, but your family stood in the way. Ever since I was born, I knew one day I would be Queen of the Realms and ruler of all the monsters. However, I never thought I'd actually get to take the crown away from you. I figured I'd have to kill you first. But forcing you to lose the throne to me before you die makes everything that much sweeter."

The dragon stomped its massive claws against the floor, carving gouges in the rock as easily as ripping paper.

"You don't want to do this," I yelled. "This thing, all

these things in here, you can't control them. They won't obey you."

"Really?" Cora laughed, the sound bouncing off the walls. The dragon dropped its head toward Declan. He widened his stance, sword ready to strike, but he didn't get the chance. The dragon swung its head like a pendulum. Declan flew into the stone wall and dropped like a heap to the floor.

"Declan," I screamed and darted toward him, but the dragon's red scaled head blocked my path. Declan's limp body moved on the ground, his harrowing moans echoing through the room.

"You're making a huge mistake," I yelled. "I don't care about the crown. You can have it. Please, just let us go."

"What do you mean, you don't want it?" Cora barked, the edge of confusion twisting her voice to a near shriek. "You're perfect, little Brea. Always thinking you're smarter than everyone else. Better than everyone else. Of course you want it."

I ran back to Aunt Becky's side and pulled her behind the skulls by the throne. Hundreds of empty eyes stared up at us. Hundreds of souls who'd never made it out of this place.

"I don't. You were right. I didn't grow up knowing who I was, and that was the luckiest thing that could've happened. You don't need to fight me. I'm not your enemy. I don't want to take what you have. I just want to protect the people I care about and live my life."

"You're lying."

"I'm not. If you want a chance to be great, come down and do it the right way. Let me give you the throne."

I stood and walked up to the head of the dragon. Its razor-sharp teeth protruded over its lip as it glared at me with its deep aquamarine eyes. My knees quaked. I held my breath and stared right back, then held up my hand. "It's not too late to end this. Come down and we can figure this out. Please trust me on this."

"Trust you? Why should I do that? You never cared about me. Not really. I was always just an accessory. But not anymore. Now I have the accessory," she tapped the crown on her head, "and I have all the power."

"But you don't want this. Not this way. You don't know the creatures that exist in here. I've seen them and I know they will betray you any chance they can. They will kill you."

"No," Cora screamed from her perch, her head whipping back and forth. "You're lying. This is a trick."

"No trick, Cora. Come down. No matter what you've done I would never want to see you die. Especially not in this place. No one deserves that."

Visions of the Sluagh flashed through my brain. Their dead breath on my skin, their claws digging into my flesh. Cora might be evil, but letting them kill her would haunt me forever.

"Forget it." She kicked her heel into the dragon's side. "Destroy her."

I ran toward the throne, but the dragon reared its head. I scrambled across the floor, trying to get out of reach, but its shadow moved the other way. It snapped at Cora, its jaw nearly clipping her arm.

"No. Her." She pointed toward me and kicked again. "Get her."

The dragon roared and the stone walls rumbled

around us. It spread its wings and flapped. Wind slammed me against the throne. Pain stabbed my spine. Cora shrieked, falling down as the dragon pushed off the ground and rose into the sky.

Crack.

Her body landed on the granite floor. I raced over and rolled her onto her back.

"Cora. Cora." I tapped the side of her face and slid my fingers to her throat. Her pulse waned but beat against my skin. Broken, but alive.

Aunt Becky and Declan joined me, staring at her unconscious body on the floor. Declan reached over and pulled the diamond crown from her head.

He held the crown out to me. "Ready to get out of here?"

I took the crown from his hands and stared at the brilliant gems. All the violence and fear for this? I placed it on my head, the weight much heavier than I expected.

White light flooded the throne room. Color faded, diluting into nothing. I slipped one hand into Declan's and one hand into Aunt Becky's, each one of them holding me together as the Midnight Realm disappeared.

White light flashed. A weightless feeling rose in my stomach until my elbows smacked the ground, my head barely missing a rock. The pure golden rays of sunshine bathed me in light and warmed my skin. The damp smell of fallen leaves and dirt.

I scrambled to my feet, the others pulling themselves up from the ground. Declan, Aunt Becky, both here and safe. Cora, however, lay in a pile of yellow leaves, not moving except for the shallow rise and fall of her chest.

Aunt Becky rushed to my side and swept me into her arms. "Oh, Brea. I didn't think I'd ever see you again."

I dug my fingers into her skin, trying to hold as tight as I could, my head buried in her shoulder inhaling her smell. That smell. The smell of home.

"Rebecca," my father's voice croaked behind us. "You're alive."

She peeled her arms from me and moved down the

line to her brother, a knowing smile gracing her lips. "Daniel."

He picked her up, her toes hovering just off the ground, and hugged her back. His cold stare melted in their embrace.

Across the clearing, Declan's crew shook his hand and played with the Lacerine, thrusting and posing as the silver blade glinted in the sunlight. He looked over at me and I stared back, our eyes locking across the clearing. I didn't know how much I owed him, but nothing I could give would ever be enough. He smiled. The kind of smile that told a story in the simple curl of a lip. A tale of bravery, and valor, and loyalty. One I would tell myself over and over until the end of time.

Then he bowed politely, his eyes still locked on mine. He dropped to his knee and lowered his head to his chest. The other nightmares watched him, and he pointed at the crown. "Bow down to your queen."

They followed Declan's lead and fell to their knees. Aunt Becky joined them, pulling my father and mother down to the ground with her.

"Please stand up, everyone," I said as my face started to burn.

I slid the crown off my head, holding it gently in my hands. The diamonds sparkled in the afternoon sun. A beautiful crown for any queen, but just not for me.

"I don't want it."

My father jumped to his feet. He took the crown from my hands and placed it back on my head. "But you are the next queen in line. If someone doesn't take the throne, the Realms will crumble and there will be chaos. Wars. No one will be safe."

"Maybe one day I will be ready. Not right now. If you want a queen that will serve the Realms with humility, grace, and love, there is no better person to hold the throne for me than Aunt Becky."

Aunt Becky scanned everyone's faces, the wrinkles around her eyes digging deep as she frowned. "I can't. I don't have any magic."

"Couldn't you have some of mine? If my parents could use their magic to bind mine, wouldn't it make sense that I could give some back?"

My father shrugged. "Perhaps it could be done. But is this really what you want?"

"Of course. There is no person I would trust more than her. And when I'm ready—if I'm ready—I will take my place and continue the line." I slipped the crown off my head again and took Aunt Becky's hand. "I just found out who I am. If you want a proper queen, I need to live more of my life and learn about this new one first."

I held the crown over Aunt Becky and rested it on her golden head. I curtsied and fell to my knee. "All hail Queen Rebecca."

Everyone returned to their knees.

"Long live the queen."

27

———

Gold and cinnamon leaves blanketed the wooded paths through Sasha's forest. The midday sun splintered through the heavy canopy of trees, helping dull the chill of the October afternoon. I held Declan's hand, my fingerless gloves only letting part of our skin touch while the rest stayed wrapped in cozy wool.

We approached the clearing, leaves falling and fluttering like confetti in the cool breeze. Declan smiled and released my hand. He marched around the circle, his heavy boots crunching through the crisp yellow grass.

He turned to me. "Looks like everything here is fine. Why did you think the portal might reopen?"

"No reason. Just wanted to be safe."

"Or maybe you just wanted a few minutes alone with me before Sasha's bonfire?" He rushed back and wrapped his arms around my waist, the tip of his nose tracing a line from between my eyes down toward my lips.

"Maybe. But weren't you the one who said you should bow before a queen?"

His eyebrows furrowed as his arms dropped from around me. "I thought you gave up that title. At least until you finish college."

"I did. Or at least I will. I still have a couple things to take care of that require being queen."

"Like what?"

I waved my finger in front of his face. "Ah, ah, ah. I don't see any kneeling."

He chuckled then took a step back and dropped down to his knee in the dirt. I ran behind a large elm tree and pulled out the Sword of the Lacerine.

"What are you doing with that thing?"

"Don't move."

I raised the blade, the sun glinting off the jewels on the hilt, and placed it on Declan's left shoulder. "I, Breanne Rosalie Vardan, Queen of the Realms, dub thee Sir Declan Noche, a knight of the fairy court and protector of the crown."

I switched from his left shoulder to his right then gently tapped the top of his head before withdrawing the sword to my side.

"Arise, Sir Noche."

Declan's dark eyes sparkled as he rose to his feet. "What was that for?"

"Because, you deserve it. You're good and true, and when I do finally take my place as Queen of the Realms, I'll need to make sure I surround myself with the right people."

"So it was a political decision?" He laughed. "And your dad still hates me."

I tugged on his sweater and pulled him closer. "Just kiss me already."

He wrapped an arm around my back and lifted me off the ground, spinning me in a circle. "It actually means a lot to me. Thank you."

"Of course. Plus, now I guess you get to be a knight-mare." I giggled and he rested me back on my feet.

"You're such a dork sometimes."

"Yup. But I think you kinda like it."

He closed his eyes and his smiled widened. The glow of the afternoon no match for his radiance. "Yeah. I kinda do."

He slid his hand to the back of my neck and tilted my head toward his lips. No monsters or demons hunted us this time. No more secrets or lies loomed in the shadows. Just a high school queen and her rebel knight writing their own fairy tale.

Thanks for reading Dreamer: A Faraway High Fairytale. Be sure to check out the next book in the series, my wild retelling of The Twelve Dancing Princesses, Fierce.

If you want to be the first to know when the next Faraway High Fairytale releases, be sure to join Scarlett's Rebel Readers for alerts straight to your inbox.

DID YOU ENJOY DREAMER?

If you enjoyed this or any of my books, please consider leaving a review or recommending it to a friend or library. A few moments to spread a positive word can be huge for an author, plus it makes me smile :)

ALSO BY SCARLETT KOL

Never miss a new release from Scarlett Kol by signing up for her newsletter at www.scarlettkol.com.

Dystopian

Mercury Rises

Paranormal

Wicked Descent

Keeper of Shadows

Sleepless

Faraway High Fairytales Series

Falling

Dreamer

Fierce

ABOUT THE AUTHOR

Born and raised in Northern Manitoba, Scarlett Kol grew up reading and writing about things that make you want to sleep with the lights on. She believed that the treasures in her mother's jewelry box were magic amulets that would give her immeasurable power and old books could transport her to secret worlds. As an adult, not much has changed. Connect with Scarlett on social media or on her website www.scarlettkol.com.

facebook.com/scarlettkolauthor

instagram.com/scarlettkol

bookbub.com/profile/scarlett-kol

amazon.com/stores/Scarlett-Kol/author/B078RZ4PWF